THE SEA TAILOR'S HANDBOOK

The Altoriae's Handbook

First published in 2025 by R. Lennard

All inquiries should be made to the author.

The characters and events portrayed in this book are fictitious or are used fictitiously. Any similarity to real persons, living or dead, is purely coincidental or unintentional.

All books in the Lissae Series are written in **UK English**.

Edited by Anna at CREATING ink.
www.CREATINGink.com

Published by Rebecca Lennard.
rlennard.com

Proofread by Ruth Dean.

Any mistakes are the fault of the author.

May the readers of the Lissae series ever have their preferred drink at the perfect temperature.

Check the trigger warnings by scanning the QR code below:

A catalogue record for this book is available from the National Library of Australia

The Altoriae's Handbook

Compiled by the

13 Altoriaes and their Guardians

To those who dwell between the Realms
and who dare to step into ones unknown
until the pages of a book are consumed,
without you, Lissae would not be the same.
I wrote this book for you.

Contents

Foreward

Handbook updated

~~*Vebaday, final week of Nightcrest 4060*~~

Shari Dawn

Re-compiled in 4062 by Samuel

Welcome to your first days protecting Lissae. This book was created from the start of my journey, as there are more creatures in the realms than I could have imagined. To that end, I began compiling my findings, so the next to take the mantle of the Altoriae will find it easier by far.

Use wisely and well, dear friends. May you have the best of luck in your lifelong task.

Jantara tar Tumaie

(Protect and Serve)

— Kay'imi

Those Who Contributed to the Handbook

Kaj'imi	Muran	Jonathan
Eminlith	AiLan	Shari
Aseudiafen Dogen	Tanika	Mitch
Metsara	Clara	Samuel
Petuar	Shael	
Thuk	Neev	
Askanar	Crista	
Quar	Aisling	
Feyla	Jali	
Raeka	Abby	
Ullmar	Tabatha	
Lerah	Resa	
Estebar	Fiona	
Liadain	Joshua	

ALTORIAES

Whilst I while away the hours, doing nothing but being, others are dying and crying all around me.

Now I have become their keeper and saviour, their confidant and friend, but ultimately, to them, I am their unknown protector.

This is what you must be, my friends. Unknown, saving the folk of Lissae. A hero who is a phenomenon does not last long at all. And we, my kin, we must last for the lifetime of this Realm.

Being the Altoriae of such a world requires certain characteristics, it is true, but being the saviour, keeper, and protector of the Realms Souls—her last defence—carries its own special burden.

Every waking moment of every single day will be beyond agony for you, my dears. You and those who have gone before you will feel the forests die, insects being crushed, and animals being slaughtered. Some days, you will find it unbearable to eat, as you can feel the pain with each bite. Have and hold your faith, my dear ones. Say thanks to your food as you know that the cycle of life must continue, and for that to happen, you must indeed eat.

Eventually, you shall find, hidden away amongst the chaos and pain, a harmony that is worthwhile hunting down. But search too hard and it shall hide from you. When it is most needed, it will arrive in an unlikely form.

One of the most important lessons that I have learned not only as an Altoriae but as a being—is to live! You cannot spend every day in training, nor can you spend each night locked in your dreams, fighting off creatures that are only bound to get more powerful as time goes on.

The townspeople of Ronah are your support and your comfort. In them, you shall find the truest friends. Their ancestors—those who I shared my life with—came to Ronah freely, knowing what I was doing and what their fate was likely to be. Yet they came in droves, so numerous that the Thorne Clan had to turn many away. These people of Ronah know what they—and you—are up against. They will support you and aid you in every endeavour that you ask them to. But you must know, my little ones, what you do is not for naught. It affects everyone in this Realm, and although a small few may know about your work, it is far better than none knowing at all.

Take care of yourself, my Altoriae. May the Deities guide and guard you and yours.

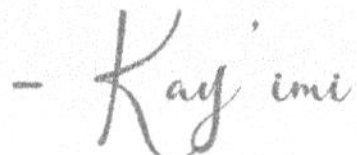

LIST OF ALTORIAES

Lissae follows a matriarchal line when choosing the next Altoriae. Perhaps in a time unrecorded, there is another Altoriae who knows our exact origins. For now, you can find the names of the Altoriaes below in bold.

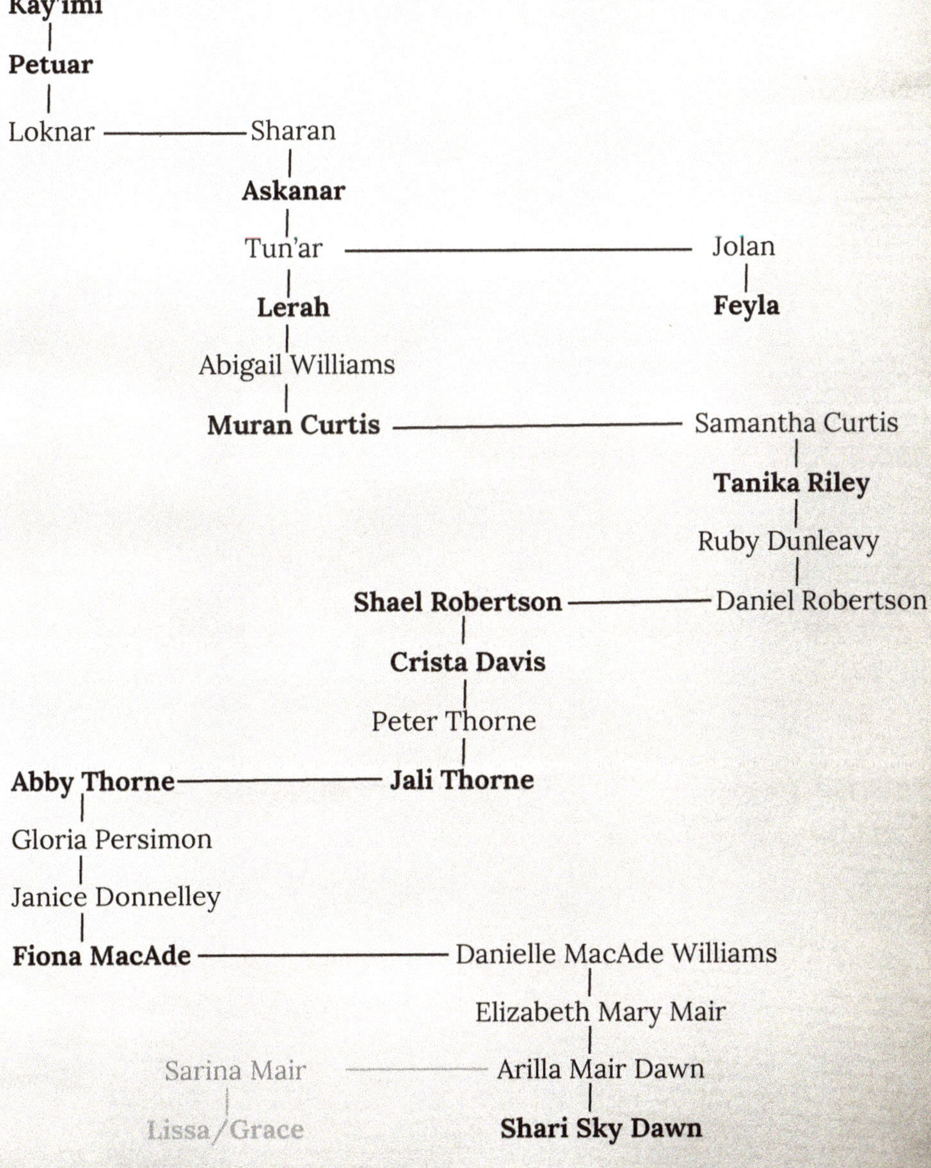

Here is my contribution to the book. Resa and I have researched and correlated the dates, ages and names of Custodians in the book—for future ease of reference, check and please add to this page.

-Fiona

Altoriae	Kay'imi	Petuar	Askanar
Guardian Name	Met'sara then Eminlith	Azulie Von Dayme then Thuk	Qar
Race	Weaver	Weaver	½ Weaver, ½ Human
Year Born	**1436**	**2342**	**3257**
Age of Becoming	406	311	90
Year of Becoming	1842	2653	3347
Age of Ending	1217	1005	121
Year of Ending	**2653**	**3347**	**3378**
Years as Altoriae	811	694	31
Age at Death	1217	1005	121
Year of Death	**2653**	**3347**	**3378**
Relation to previous Altoriae	First Altoriae	Daughter	Grand-daughter
Altoriae Number	1	2	3
Loss of Life via	Ambush	Accident	Attack

Altoriae	Feyla	Lerah	Muran Curtis
Guardian Name	Unnamed Ullmar	Estebar	Liadain
Race	½ Weaver, ½ Human	½ Weaver, ½ Human	½ Weaver, ½ Human
Year Born	**3318**	**3351**	**3685**
Age of Becoming	60	120	5
Year of Becoming	3378	3471	3690
Age of Ending	153	334	45
Year of Ending	**3471**	**3685**	**3730**
Years as Altoriae	93	214	40
Age at Death	153	334	45
Year of Death	**3471**	**3685**	**3730/4059**
Relation to previous Altoriae	Grand-daughter	½ sister	Grand-son
Altoriae Number	4	5	6
Loss of Life via	Other Means	Attack	Attack

Altoriae	Tanika Riley	Shael Robertson	Crista Davis
Guardian Name	Ailan	Clara	Neev
Race	¼ Weaver, ¾ Human	Weaver	½ Weaver, ½ Human
Year Born	**3740**	**3786**	**3845**
Age of Becoming	5	4	14
Year of Becoming	3745	3790	3859
Age of Ending	46	73	32
Year of Ending	**3786**	**3859**	**3877**
Years as Altoriae	41	69	18
Age at Death	46	73	32
Year of Death	**3786**	**3859**	**3877**
Relation to previous Altoriae	Niece	Great Niece	Daughter
Altoriae Number	7	8	9
Loss of Life via	Natural Causes	Accident	Attack

Altoriae	Jali Thorne	Abby Thorne	Fiona MacAde
Guardian Name	Aisling	Tabatha	Resa Sunab
Race	¼ Weaver, ¾ Human	¼ Weaver, ¾ Human	Weaver
Year Born	**3861**	**3871**	**3971**
Age of Becoming	16	9	10
Year of Becoming	3877	3880	3981
Age of Ending	19	91	24
Year of Ending	**3880**	**3971**	**3995**
Years as Altoriae	3	82	14
Age at Death	19	91	24
Year of Death	**3880**	**3971**	**3995**
Relation to previous Altoriae	Grand-daughter	Sister	Great Grand-daughter
Altoriae Number	10	11	12
Loss of Life via	Accident	Attack	Attack

Altoriae	Shari Dawn	Grace
Guardian Name	Jonathan Buan	
Race	½ Ilutri, ½ Human	Human
Year Born	**4042**	4038
Age of Becoming	4	22
Year of Becoming	4046	4060
Age of Ending	18	
Year of Ending	**4060**	
Years as Altoriae	14	
Age at Death		
Year of Death		
Relation to previous Altoriae	Great Great Niece	Cousin
Altoriae Number	13	14
Loss of Life via		

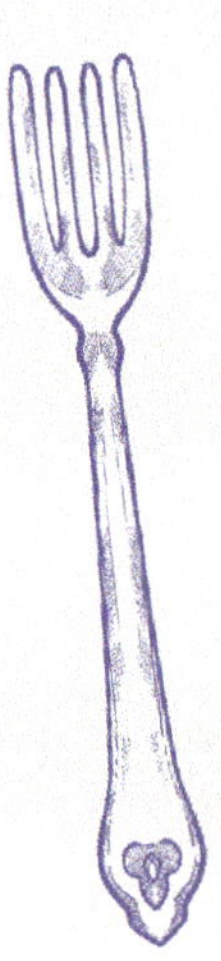

The past Altoriaes have lived very rich and fulfilling lives, however short they may have been. Their experiences and yours help the future generations. For as we get stronger, so do the ones we must fight to protect our Realm. As the years go by, it is up to you, the Altoriae, to correlate and record your tragedies and triumphs. Do this without fail, loved ones, and we shall forever live on.

CONDUCT

The Altoriae is someone others look to in times of need and in times where hope is rarely found. As such, the Altoriae must conduct herself appropriately at all times.

The rules of Conduct include:

Using reasonable force to prevent a soul on or from Lissae from injury.

Protecting the inhabitants of Lissae above all others first.

Trying, when possible, to use non-violent methods to dissuade beings from entering Lissae. If that fails, try to use non-lethal methods to dissuade the said beings. And if you do not succeed, any threat to Lissae must be removed before it reaches our gateway. Use reasonable force to terminate a soul who means our Realm harm.

Uphold your duties to the best of your ability.

Know when you are weakened—ask your Guardian to help you protect our Realm.

Treat others on our Realm with kindness and compassion—no matter how thick-headed they may seem.

Maintain your silence about who you are for as long as you can. Once it becomes known who an Altoriae is, expect much more forceful attacks, many of which may occur on Lissae rather than on the Realms.

Use of your abilities on residents of Lissae for vengeful means is punishable by banishment to the outer Realms. Do so at your own risk.

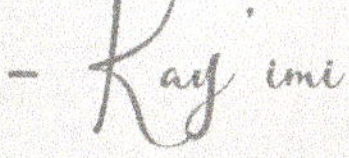

DUTIES

The Altoriae's duties

First and Foremost: Protecting the Realm

Secondly: Protecting Ronah and her residents

Thirdly: Calling Ronah's residents to arms in times of need

Fourthly: Teaching Ronah's residents

Fifthly: Maintaining peace on Ronah

Sixthly: Ensuring that Ronah's young remember their Elder's pledges to the Altoriae

And Seventhly: Maintaining the Altoriae's Handbook for the use of future Altoriaes

Ronah's Duties to the Altoriae

First and Foremost: Ensuring a safe place for the Altoriae to live

Secondly: Ensuring a safe place for the Altoriae to train

Thirdly: Maintaining peace amongst the residents to the best of her abilities

Fourthly: Training the Altoriae if asked

And Fifthly: Guiding and guarding the Altoriae when no Guardian is available

Pledged Duties to the Altoriae may vary greatly, and as such they are to be recorded here for future reference. They may be renewed or changed from one Altoriae to the next, therefore only the most up to date are kept.

All new residents of Ronah must agree to the following duties; otherwise, they must find somewhere else to reside.

Ronah's Residents' Duties to the Altoriae

First and Foremost: To protect the Altoriae at all costs
Secondly: To assist the Altoriae in any way she asks
Thirdly: Answering an Altoriae's call without hesitation
Fourthly: Ensuring a safe place for the Altoriae to train
Fifthly: Maintaining peace amongst Ronah's residents to the best of their abilities

Clans may pledge certain duties to the Altoriae as well. Current pledges include:

The Thorne Clan

First and Foremost: To assist the Altoriae in any way she asks
Secondly: Answering an Altoriae's call without hesitation
Thirdly: Ensuring a safe place for the Altoriae to train
Fourthly: Protecting Ronah
Fifthly: Protecting Ronah's residents
And Sixthly: Ensuring Ronah's young remember their Elders' pledges to the Altoriae

The Ribeck Clan

First and Foremost: To protect the Altoriae at all costs
Secondly: Answering an Altoriae's call without hesitation
Thirdly: Ensuring a safe place for the Altoriae to train
Fourthly: Training the Altoriae if asked
Fifthly: Ensuring Ronah's young remember their Elders' pledges to the Altoriae
And Sixthly: Maintaining peace amongst Ronah's residents to the best of their abilities

SECRECY & INSTINCT

The Altoriae's identity must be kept secret for as long as possible. The Altoriae's Guardian and immediate family may know, but no others.

Do not tell people one at a time. Tell multiple people simultaneously, or risk losing those closest to you.

There are beings and creatures who know how to search out secrets, and they are constantly scanning for an individual who knows the identity of Lissae's Altoriae.

Until their methods change—tell no one!

Once your secret is revealed, you can rest easier knowing that those you trust won't be the only beings who are targeted.

Now, it will be everyone.

***

Although Instinct is a huge part of an Altoriae's make-up—do not rely on it. Train every day, in every situation, on as many Realms as you can make it to. Having your instincts tell you that something is wrong is no good if you can't do anything to fix it.

In some aspects, our instincts help, such as when we meet our Guardian. A part of us already knows they'll be right, even before it's made formal. We must abide by the tests, pomp and circumstances for the sake of the Elders.

Keep in mind that there's nothing that says we can't angle the tests to ensure our chosen candidate wins.

In other cases, our instincts may hinder. There are beings across the Realm who know how to manipulate your mind, and will not hesitate to do so. This is why you must train. Don't let the blood of your family decorate the walls of the place you called home. Don't be like me.

Notes & Observations

Kay'imi

Successes

Created *The Altoriae's Handbook*, without which, we would all be lost.

Failures

She told one of her friends her identity as Lissae's protector before she informed the town, and her friend was found in her bed, ripped to shreds by some demon in the night.

Since then, the Altoriae tells no one who she is until the proper training is completed. Solitary, untrained people who hold secrets and walk the Realms may still hold on to their confidences, but seldom do they hold on to their lives.

Killers

Kay'imi was ambushed by the Ahana and killed by a lone Innarnian Archer.

Allies

One member of the Thorne family has carried this pendant since Kay'imi first gave it to Eminlith, her Guardian. Eminlith went on to marry the first Thorne who arrived on Ronah. His name was Timony. So enthralled with Eminlith was he, that he made a vow to Kay'imi that the Thorne family would forever protect the Altoriae and her Guardian. To this day, the Thorne Clan keeps Timony's promise. And yet, over time, it has been added too. We have sworn to protect the people of Ronah, and Ronah itself. The ruby red pendant is a symbol of all the love, care and protection. One that embodies all the Thornes who have ever sacrificed their lives to save any that we defend. It will protect our Realm and our Island as surely as we have protected the Altoriae.

Notes

I do not know what to think.

For months now, it feels like a pressure has been building just behind the front of my ribs. I was just outside the forest today, watching Shania's child run around and fight invisible monsters, when a very real creature broke through the thicket and tried to grab Hensey.

I reacted without thought. A ball of plasma left my hand and slammed through the skull of the creature. Hensey screamed, and honestly, I wanted to as well.

Instead, I let the plasma flow from me and burn away the creature's corpse. I wished the child had never seen such a thing. A wisp of green floated up from the ground, and Hensey blinked twice before going back to his game.

I threw a ward around the clearing and sat, shaken.

A voice filled my head, one so old and motherly. I instantly felt at ease.

I won't share the details here but suffice to say that Lissae asked me to watch over her. To protect her.

And I will. So the next Hensey will never have to face a situation like that again.

How does Lissae expect me to do this job alone? There are more than minutes in a day, and only one of me. Every being on the Realms seems to be keen to step into our borders, looking only for their own gain. Each night, I patrol, and each day I smile and pretend I am not exhausted to my soul. I do not know how long I can continue this farce.

Shania is dead. And it's my fault.

Lissae warned me—told me not to tell anyone what she had asked of me. But I told Shania. Warlon just sent to me to say she'd been ripped to shreds in their bed. He wanted to warn me. along with everyone else of Ronah.

It's my fault.

This may be my last entry.

Was stabbed.

Through heart.

Dying.

You'll have to forgive Kayimi. She's ever so dramatic. She's fine—just needs a week of bedrest.

That was Met'sara. Lissae above and below. she's. a pain.

A pain who saved you.

True. She will forever have my thanks.

And your back.

It's official. Met'sara is my Guardian, and the whole of Ronah knows I am their mysterious protector.

Met'sara was injured during a skirmish on Earra. I have never been so scared. I must make something that will keep her from harm.

My diary has turned into something more. A place for all the information I've gathered across the realms. After my brief encounter with death, I spoke with Lissae, who confirmed that, upon my passing, a new Altoriae will be chosen.

If you are my replacement, Well met. I hope you find some wisdom in my words worth holding on to.

Met'sara is dead. She stepped between me and a beastly being — something bigger than I've seen before. Three eyes and silver scales all over, apart from the wings. Great leathery things, capable of blowing a fulni off its feet. Two powerful hind legs, and arms that end in wickedly sharp claws. This beast was at least three Lissaen's tall.

We shifted into Rataeo to investigate a disturbance, when the being dropped from the sky. It growled something I couldn't understand. A demand, perhaps, from the tone. When I didn't move fast enough, it lunged.

I know not of what instinct prompted Met'sara, but she seemed to know the beast better than I. She shoved me to the side, and I watched, powerless, as it bit her in half before my eyes.

My beautiful Guardian, gone.

I have yet to tell her mate. Or her children. Darulia has one on the way, and I loathe to put further stress on her, and yet, it must be done. The not knowing is worse.

The conversations went about as well as expected. I ache, all over. My wounds have yet to heal. I fear the psychic scars Met'sara's passing has left far more of a mark on me.

The Elders are saying I need a new Guardian.

Rubbish. I was fine by myself. I will continue to be fine.

I am not fine.

Tomorrow, after I lick my wounds, I shall start the search. I fear none shall compare to Met'sara, however hard they may try.

Lissae has suggested some sort of trial, to judge the new Guardian's abilities. Who am I to argue with a realm?

Apparently, taking all the candidates into an active war zone without determining their skills first is not a good idea.

Nor is seeing if they can cross erupting volcanoes. How was I supposed to know that none of them were healers?

Lissae thinks I'm being 'bitter' and 'spiteful' and 'not giving the candidates a fair chance.' She's turned the task over to the Elders.

At least they've chosen someone who is somewhat competent. Meet Eminlith. She, and her apprentice, are to guard and guide me.

Well met

Well met. I am Azulie.

I do not understand other beings. How do I make enemies so easily?

Your sparkling personality?

Rude.

Patrols are increasing again, as are instances of Lissaens not returning home. Someone from the Dark realms appears to not be happy with us.

The upper Grey Realms are no longer safe. The Ducibus won't let my patrollers past the second level. I fear that, should the dissent continue, Lissae will be cut off. I am not sure Eminlith is safe. I will continue to work on the device I was making before.

Eminlith discovered a rogue, gaseous form in the Portal. She single-handedly drove it back. When she awakens, I must give her my congratulations. And thanks.

Today, I gave Eminlith the pendant I've been working on. It should keep her safe as we traverse worlds in order to protect the ones dearest to us.

I'm getting old, I fear. My swing is slower, and my Innarn seems to need more concentration than before. What happens when an Altoriae grows to be an elder?

We shall never know. Kay'imi was on patrol today, this year of 2653. She was felled by a lone Ahana archer after an ambush. May she walk into Immosa with her head high and her bow by her side.

Petuar

Notes

I am both honoured and terrified that Lissae sought me to be her next great protector. All my life, I have basked in my mother's shadow, learning everything she had to offer in order to lead the patrols she could not. Never, in my wildest dreams, did I think that I would end up as her replacement.

I miss her.

I begged her to stop, but she was stubborn. When Dad called for help on patrol, she went, instead of me.

It should have been me.

I got there moments after she did. Watched the arrow tip emerge from my father's throat. Screamed as the next flew before his body dropped. It embedded in her heart, the poison stopping it before I could shift her back to Lissae.

Losing one parent is bad enough, but having them both killed before you, on the same night, is brutal.

Yet, I must find the strength to carry on. To tell the Elders that their first Altoriae has fallen, and I have taken her place.

When Lissae called, I answered. Just as my mother did.

It is a task I never wanted to do.

The Realms are quiet tonight. There is a feeling in the air, as if every being has drawn in a breath, but has yet to let it out. The pressure builds, and I dread what is to happen when it pops.

It popped. Eminlith caught the brunt of it, and Azulie, her apprentice, now holds the title she's been training for so long.

I wish I had been quicker. Reached her sooner.

Instead, I tripped over her body, desecrating her corpse with cedore slime, and screamed like a child with a bug in their bed.

Some Altoriae I am.

Do you know what makes it all worse? Azulie must now choose her own replacement, while she still sees Eminlith's half-melted face every time she closes her eyes.

Not helpful.

Well met to Thuk. who has become Azulie's apprentice. May your learnings be long and drawn out.

    Petuar!

I have come to the realisation that. one day. Azulie shall be writing how I die. This leaves me with a choice. I can wallow. or I can record as many things about the Realms as possible in order to ensure that my replacement never has to wonder what they might come across on their travels.

Azulie is quite the artist. Her sketches adorn the pages of what is rapidly becoming a tome. A tradition to continue for those who follow. perhaps?

Never shall some believe the sights I have seen. the deeds I have performed. Please. young ones. do not misunderstand an old. tired warrior's words. My life has not been filled with danger and intrigue as some may claim. but of tedious chores and annoying disturbances to clear up.

    During my time as Altoriae. I have endured many attempts by various different entities-both Dark and Light-to infiltrate Lissae. So many attempts. too many to keep track of. but one stands out in my mind

There's a race of extraordinarily Dark beings that inhabit the Darkest of Realms. I hope you, dear one, never meet them. They are—and forgive me, I know your training goes against this, but—they are evil. They thrive in chaos. Sunlight hurts their innermost essence. They feast on the souls of others, and as they devour these souls, they cause an unbelievable amount of pain—almost as if they are tearing chunks out of your flesh. How do I know this?

They tried to consume Lissae.

These creatures are called Q'Aralide.

There is an especially nasty one. He (well, I assume it's a 'he') is golden in colour. He is the priest who led the attack on Lissae. From what I have been able to ascertain, he is only part Q'Aralide—the other part I am not sure of, except that it is humanoid, which is how he managed to get into our Realm.

Nothing would surprise me as to the lengths this one would go to, to return to our fair Realm.

Azulie passed away in her sleep, peacefully. May we all go the same way.

Thuk took over as Guardian some moons back, when it became obvious that Azulie's advanced age was catching up with her. It is still odd to know that she will never again fight by my side or berate me for getting wounded, even as she stitches me back together. I will miss her greatly.

I wish for peace, although I doubt I shall see it. The days of our gateway being bombarded constantly seem to be done, but I fear the lull is a ruse, designed to test my patience. It is taking every ounce of sense to stop from storming the surrounding Realms and expanding our borders so we may be safer.

Not that we have the people power to hold such territory for long, nor would it be fair on our mostly peaceful neighbours. Perhaps it is time to hang up the sword and attempt diplomacy?

Turns out I'm not much of a diplomat.
Is that why we're at war with Gerhar?

Not the only reason why.
Huh, look at that. I can tell you're sulking just through your writing.

Thuk!

It is my distinct displeasure to inform you that Petuar, daughter of Kay'imi and second Altoriae, died this night of 3347 due to an unfortunate accident.

Askanar

Successes

Creator of the Veti Cant, a particularly complicated sign language that is known only to those who have helped Altoriaes. Some beings also choose to teach the Cant to their descendants so they may continue to help the Altoriae.

Notes

Grandmother died tripping over a fallen axe, and no one wants to mention it.

I woke last night to a howl so loud that even I heard it. Thuk's Innarn must have been amplifying his lungs, because normally noise does not reach my ears.

Before he'd even finished, another voice filled my head. Lissae.

Asking me to replace Grandmother as her Altoriae. Me.

Hers is a legacy I never thought I could aspire to, but I will train every day to make her proud.

Thuk stayed as long as he could, but grief took him far too soon. I've long suspected his heart would follow

Grandmother when she left, assuming he wouldn't fall victim to an arrow first.

Qar is now my Guardian. May we retain our titles until the Final Sleep claims us both.

Using Innarn to hear is such a waste when I'm on the battlefield. There may be less fighting now than there was for the first Altoriae, but I fear that the split in my concentration will lead to an undesirable end.

Qar suggested turning hand-speech into code. Something only we could understand. I wonder how well that would work on the battlefield?

Creating a whole new language from scratch is ridiculous. Why did I think this was a good idea?

I met a young Wikkur today by the name of Jerran. He was lost, wandering the Realms alone. I know the reputation held by most of his race, but I'll not turn a child away when they're in need.

There's something odd, though. I wonder if it's my own grasp of spoken language, but he couldn't understand me. Qar thinks it could be because Jerran was so much younger than the normal refugees, but I'm not convinced. I found a friendly family of Ferah to watch over him and promised I'd check in when I can.

Visiting Jerran is a delightful break from the monotony of patrol.

You're becoming attached.
I have my own family at home to contend with. I do not need another soul to watch over.

And yet, you are.

Hush, Qar.

Jerran has hearing loss! It explains so much. I've started teaching him the Cant. We've called it the Veti Cant, in honour of his fallen sister.

I must caution against this, Askanar.
Hush, Qar. I am eager to teach him more.

Patrolling has kicked up a notch. We've had three injuries in the last week. It seems like whatever break our oppressors where on is over.

It's been months since I've seen Jerran. I'll have to make a special trip.

It was a trap. They were waiting for her. Now we all wait for the announcement of the new Altoriae.

Feyla

Successes

Mapping the Realms into their bands and sub-levels.

Notes

Introducing Feyla, granddaughter of Askanar, and the newest
Attoriae of Lissac.

So I'm meant to write in this?

Yes.

And if I don't want to?

Consider it part of your training.

Ugh.

Survived the first month. Thuk did not.   is now my Guardian.

Survived the first year. How lucky.

Still here three years later.

I used the Handbook last night to look up the beings of Attum. I suppose I can see the value of it now.

Why do we have to record *everything*? Is it not better to let actions speak for themselves? The stories of my grandmother are still going strong

I found out today that children are being told Kay'imi was taken down by an army. I swear I can hear Thuk laughing at me all the way from Immosa.

Fine. I'll write in the book.

Suppose I should tell   about it too.

3398

Feyla is a being of the sword, not the quill, and has tasked me with recording our notes in the Handbook. Well met, avid reader. I am

, Guardian (and scribe) of the fourth Altoriae.

3398

Patrolling is happening at regular intervals now—at least twice a week. On the days that we don't have to guard the gateway, Feyla likes to explore. So far, we've mapped most of the gateways on the same sub-level as us, and we are aiming to add to the crude map we have constructed.

By we, means I.

Well, I could not have done this without your help. I would have died seven times over!

Exactly.

3418

It has taken two decades, but we have thoroughly investigated every single Grey Realm in all three bands. I humbly suggest that we next tackle the third band of Light Realms.

Sure.

3420

Our biggest challenge at the moment is not patrols, as the attacks have reduced once more, but gaining access to the higher bands. I can see them when I stand in a particular spot in the Portal and look out of the corner of my eye, but I struggle to move into the Lighter or Darker Realms. Feyla, of course, has no such issue. She is reluctant to talk about what she finds and is even less inclined to write the information down.

3422

Finally, Feyla found a way to bring me along when she travels to the Light Realms. They are so different from the Grey Realms, I fear it will take decades just to do the third band.

3442

The third band is finished. Feyla is refusing to take me to the second band. I must change her mind.

3443

Feyla's mind was not changed.
        turned on his Altoriae.
    And I turned on him before Lissae even had a chance to ask.

Who am I? Ullmar, Feyla's new Guardian, appointed directly after I stabbed the sanctimonious twit who thought he knew better than the Altoriae. His name has been scrubbed from the Handbook and will not be spoken again.

3444

It seems that the Realms are becoming quiet again. There are no dates or references to time when this happened last, so I know not if it follows a pattern or remains a fluke of the seasons. Whatever the reason, it is good to be able to relax for a short while.

I spoke too soon.

The Realms are in an uproar. A Dark Realm of the third band is causing strife and their victims are mounting. I fear the Portal has become more of a morgue with bodies lining the walls. Feyla has been patrolling relentlessly.

Well met, Estebar, who has gladly become my apprentice.

Well met.

3445

Perhaps it is seasonal? Quiet descends again and allows us time to lick our wounds. I must try to convince Feyla to maintain the patrols, lest the same thing happen.

The quiet means that we are able to finish off the maps. The Ducibus have no problem with me going to the Lightest of Realms but refuse to allow me below the first band of Dark Realms. Instead, I have asked Pala to pass the map around for all the Ducibus guarding the doorways to write their Realms in.

This method has proven quite successful and I'm pleased to say that by this time next month, the map should be finished and I'll be able to enter it into the Handbook.

My prediction was correct. The map of the Realms is complete. Feyla is most happy to report back on the places she's visited, and we hope that you will continue to add to the information to help those who come next.

3471

Feyla is... gone.

I can feel her through the bond, but she has disappeared. Totally untraceable. I have searched for months, pretending that she in on extended patrol, and all for naught.

She does not feel distressed, but she is fading.

Tonight, Lissae spoke to me for the first time.

"Feyla can no longer fulfil her duties. It is time for a new Altoriae."

And so, I too, will step down, leaving the Realm to Estebar and the fifth Altoriae.

You both have my best wishes and solemn condolences.

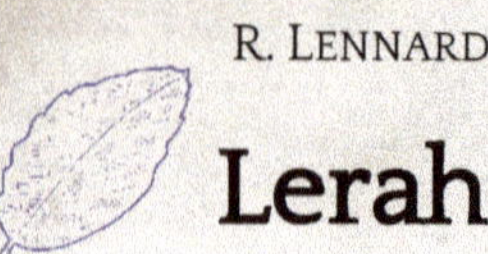

Lerah

Notes

The night after Lissae asked me to be the new Altoriae, Ullmar thrust this book at me and I knew that Feyla was lost to us.

I shall forever miss my sister, and I refuse to stop hunting for the thing that took her.

3675

I have poured through the Handbook and suppose I should introduce myself. Greetings and well met. I am Lerah, half-sister to the fourth Altoriae. I currently hold the title of the fifth Altoriae. Estebar is my Guardian.

Well met.

It is odd to think that, at 120 years of age, I am to become the Realm's protector. My children are still in school. I feel like I should be worrying more about grades and what's for dinner, instead of patrol schedules and which weapon is the best to use on Karara.

I've trained, of course. With the Realm the way it is, it would be stupid not to. I ~~was~~ was Feyla's sparring partner for years. I remain grateful to Estebar for his knowledge. He helped to map the Realms, and without him, I wouldn't know the difference between Duhiomel and Damiuth.

It is my honour to help and guide you.

Only six months in, and already the curse of the Altoriae has hit.

Cian is dead.

Killed.

All because he knew I was the Altoriae.

My husband. Gone.

And all I want to do is burn the Realms to ash.

Lerah is fine, just a little singed.

She attempted to go after her husband's assassin but forgot Air and Fire shouldn't mix. The Air Innarnian who sent Cian to the Spirit Realm fed Lerah's Fire until she could no longer control it.

Thank Lissae. I found her in time.

She will spend the next week recovering in the Healers Centre, and if she so much as twitches a toe wrong, I will have them extend her time. Her children do not deserve to lose both parents.

I do not deserve a Guardian like Estebar. He's done far more than ensure the patrols go ahead. I was so worried about the children, but he stepped in without a word and was just. . . there.

Even with training, it is so easy to let emotions run over, to rush into battle screaming instead of taking that precious moment before to think, plan and adapt to our opponents. I beg you, don't make the same mistake I did.

3480

Patrolling remains constant. We've added to the information about the Realms, which you should continue to do as well, if you follow me.

I've been pouring over the Handbook, and the personal diaries of the past Altoriaes, and it feels like Lissae is picking us from the same lineage. It makes me worry—will my children be called to fight when I am gone?

They are not ready. School is finished for the eldest, but there are still three to finish, and all of them girls. What if they are chosen?

I've spoken to Estebar, and he agrees. We must start training them.

3485

If I could go back in time and start training my babies sooner, I would. Aleria came on patrol with me last week, and now she lies, unresponsive, in the Healers Centre.

It is not your fault.

Except it is. The only consolation is the one who tried to take her life breathes no more.

Poetic

No, it was bloody, and drawn out. Just as he deserved.

Lerah.

What?

Aleria woke up! Although, she must still be confused. She said a cloud attacked her. Either way, she is back with the living.

We must step up her training and ensure that this never happens again.

3502

Aleria moved to the mainland, stating that she couldn't bear the thought of being attacked again. She said the training was too much, which is ridiculous. Her sisters haven't complained.

Yet.

Are you questioning my methods, Estebar?

No, Altoriae.

The capsule ferrying Aleria and her goods crashed and was lost to the waves. The Wisara are searching, but I fear for her survival. And what it means for Lerah if she does not make it.

My fears were founded. May Aleria walk into Immosa with her head high and her staff by her side.

My remaining children have grown, and I am now a grandmother. It is gratifying, however delayed, to know that my girls are now training their own children. Funny how you change when the fear of a loved one motivates you.

There have been some unsavoury characters sniffing around the castle, trying to discover our secrets. I will have to ward the book to discourage them from snooping.

Seems that I became an author overnight. If you happen to pick up a copy of The Sea Tailor's Handbook and the cover shimmers in your hands, commiserations/ congratulations—you're the Altoriae. May you last longer than the rest of us.

I swear that there are times when the Realms all go on holidays at the same time. I've been doing this for long enough to know that there's no rhyme or reason, just enough time for you to become complacent before they ramp up the attacks again.

I'm a grandmother again. I do not know if I'll have the time to see the child before the break is over, but Esteban tells me that my grandchild is happy and healthy.

The child has a name.

The last time I wrote my child's name in this book, she died.

Lerah. I promise to keep them all safe.

I know. Sometimes, fate has other plans for us.

I'll protect you all from the fates.

Somewhere, as soon as I wrote that, the fates laughed. The night Lerah's grandchild was born, she was travelling home to see him and was attacked right outside our own gateway.

In the morning, I will petition Pala to see if he will allow the Altoriae and her Guardian to shift directly in and out. No one should be killed outside their front door.

Muran Curtis

Killers

Anriluka, a U'tan from Rataeo, decimated the population of Ronah by tracking the Altoriae to his home. She did so by striking when her victims were asleep, ripping their souls from their bodies, and then returning and feeding on their flesh.

During one such incident, the Altoriae intervened. Anriluka was expecting him and managed to overpower and kill him. Muran's Guardian harnessed the power of the elders and banished Anriluka back to Rataeo.

The only way she can return is if Lissae lasts long enough to have a thirteenth Altoriae.

Notes

I held the Realm as long as I could. Now it is up to you, Muran. May you live long and fight as fiercely as your grandmother did. Liadain will be your Guardian.

Well met, young Altoriae.

I am not sure I knew what I was signing up for when I agreed to be Estebar's apprentice. There was never any mention of training a five-year-old, yet here we are.

Muran, I must admit, is not like other children. He's quite happy to play by himself, but his games involve lobbing Innarn at unsuspecting onlookers.

So far, no one has been injured. If I bring the possibility up with his mother, she shrugs and mutters something about training harder.

The fruit fell close to Lerah's tree, that's for sure.

I've put together a simple patrolling schedule to keep the elders happy. As far as the rest of Lissae is concerned, we don't have an Altoriae at the moment, and we won't until I deem the child in my care ready.

Muran is a quick study. I wonder how much of his training is done while I'm away. Lissae is a notorious taskmaster, according to Lerah. I do feel that she embellished somewhat in order to get her children to train even when they didn't want to. Goodness knows that sometimes I need the motivation.

There are times when I'm in the Portal, or off-Realm, and I feel like Muran is right behind me, just out of reach. When I get home, he's safely in his bed. I swear my instincts are playing up.

Turns out I was right. There's nothing quite like the look on a nine-year-old's face when you inform him that his mother knows he sneaks out at night.

He didn't believe me until we got back and she broke down. I feel bad, but the Realms are no place for a child so young.

Training continues to go well. At only thirteen, Muran is more than capable of knocking me off my feet.

I regret to say that it's almost time we announced that he is the Altoriae. We've never been without one before—it's always happened immediately after the last Altoriae passed. I do wonder if there's something wrong with Lissae. Her sends are less frequent, and the seasons these last few years seem to drag on a tad longer than they should, even on the Shifting Islands. The Wisara talk about how mainlander farmers are having difficulty with crop rotation and harvests not being ready at the usual time.

I've asked Lissae if there's anything wrong, but she refuses to answer me. Maybe Muran will have more luck when he's older.

3705

At 15 years old, Muran Curtis of Ronah becomes the youngest official Altoriae of Lissae. He's breaking all sorts of records, including being the only male Altoriae to date. No one is quite sure what to make of him, and he's loving every moment.

Our first official patrol is tonight and should he survive, I shall turn the Handbook over to him.

Well met. I am Muran, sixth Altoriae.

3710

There are rumours of a rogue U'tan disturbing the lower Grey Realms.

Apparently, she cleared out a nest of pteradiles. I can't see what's so bad about that—she's basically doing our job for us.

I rescind my earlier statement. She is a menace who goes by the name Anriluka. Something about that U'tan is deeply unsettling. I have advised Muran to stay as far away from her as he can get.

3711

I don't know why I expected him to listen. Of course, he didn't. Our most esteemed Altoriae decided to take on Anriluka. By himself. Without informing anyone.

It's not like I waltzed up to her, tapped her on the tentacle and asked her to dance without expecting backlash. I knew she'd react like that.

You knew she'd try to rend your flesh to get to "the good bits"?

Not exactly...

You, sir, are grounded.

I'm not 5 anymore, Liadain. It's time you let me take care of Lissae properly.

You can take care of Lissae when you stop taking needless risks.

There's nothing quite like being told off in writing that will be read by those yet to come. Please forgive Liadain. She's a tad stressed at the moment.

Anriluka is trouble; there's no doubt about it. Pray that I am able to defeat her and that she is never around to bother you.

3728

She's found her way onto Lissae. One by one, my people are going missing, and I'm never quite fast enough to catch her.

We've decided not to tell the townsfolk, lest it cause undue panic. I'm not a fan of this plan, but I understand Liadain's concerns. We aim to catch her quickly, but so far, we haven't had much luck.

3730

She went too far. Anriluka killed Ronah's Linked right in front of her son. As soon as I left to track her down, she came back and killed him too. May they both enter Immosa with their heads held high.

I swear I will see the end of this beast, even if it kills me.

3730

It did. Kill him.

Anriluka's days are numbered. Just wait, beast. I will track you down and avenge my Altoriae.

Although it took longer than I wanted, Anriluka is now dead. As is a full third of Ronah's residents. More have fled to the mainland to escape Anriluka's reign of terror, and I can't blame them one bit.

With Muran gone, it's best that I introduce my apprentice. It will be up to you to keep the Realm safe until the next Altoriae is found.

Well met, dear ones. I am Ailan.

3742

Muran's death was a blow to Liadain that I don't think she ever recovered from. May they find each other and the peace they so greatly deserve in Immosa.

Tanika Riley

Successes

Created a safe space for inter-Realm refugees.

Killers

Died of natural causes.

Notes

3745

Lissae announced her new Altoriae to me while I was dodging a chakram. I'm absolutely sure there is a rule against that.

Anyway, welcome, Tanika. May you outlive your predecessors and spend most nights in your comfortable bed.

She, ah, can't write yet. She's five.

Tanika might not be able to write, but she can swing a sword better than most adults.

Muran had been teaching his niece how to wield weapons since she was old enough to pick them up, and Lissae has been whispering to the child as she sleeps, stealing her into a dreamscape to teach her Innarn.

If she weren't the Altoriae, I would be concerned.

3752

Well met. I am Tanika, the seventh Altoriae. I am twelve years old and ready to defend the Realm, no matter what Ailan says.

You are still too young to come on patrol, no matter how neatly you write in the Handbook.

Mean.

One day you'll thank me.

3755

Finally. I get to go on patrol. I can't wait to report back.

Ailan. I'm sorry. You were right. I never want to patrol again.

I'm so sorry, Tanika. Next time will be better.

Next time was not better. Tanika is staying in the Healers Centre overnight. I worry that this might be too much for her. I've started the search for an apprentice, just in case saving the Realm calls back to me again.

3756

I am feeling like the worst Guardian of all time. Three of my apprentices fell within weeks of each other. Maybe the tests are a good idea after all.

3759

Test completed. Apprentice found.

Well met, Altoriac.

Well met, Clara. Does this mean I don't have to patrol anymore?

Only occasionally, now. I can use the time to train Clara to better protect and guide you.

Excellent.

3762

Clara's training has gone well. I barely need to patrol now. Ailan has been kind enough to let me take on the more diplomatic side of the role, which is arguably harder than stabbing beings.

There are more than a few refugees who are seeking shelter within Lissae. I've asked the Council of Elders if there would be room on the mainland for them. So far, their response has been lacklustre, but I am determined that everyone should feel safe—and Lissae is the safest Realm around.

3765

I am grateful for Ailan's training. Without it, I would never have been able to make a new continent. Now, there is more than enough room for refugees from across the Realms to live safely.

They must all be tested to make sure they wish us no ill will.

Of course, Ailan, I'm not that trusting.

I've devised a test for those seeking refuge on Lissae. I'm sure it's fool proof.

Honestly, it feels like if you write something in this book, the opposite is cursed to happen.

Tanika is in the Healers Centre, again.

This time, it's due to one of the 'refugees' giving her poisoned fruit.

Of course, we've had plenty of legitimate beings settle on the new continent without any fuss. But there just had to be one who wrecked it for the rest, didn't there?

The Healers think Tanika will be out in a few days. I can but hope.

3778

What sort of Altoriae needs a walking stick?

Me.

I'm that sort of Altoriae.

Although it was years ago, whatever poison was in that fruit did odd things to my insides. I can feel my body failing. It's harder to move, slower in rising, and my aim, which I perfected at five, has been off for the last six months. The Healers are saying something about the poison attaching my connective tissue, whatever that is. Nothing I can poke a sword at, at any rate.

Instead, I tramp around with a quarterstaff and claim that being prepared is the only reason why I hold it with a shaking, white-knuckled grip.

Some Altoriae I am.

3786

Tanika was far too clever for her own good. She hid the book from me. Said she was doing research. I never got to read her last message before it was too late.

May she be finally able to throw away that staff and walk into Immosa on her own two feet.

Clara and I will look after Lissae until the next Altoriae is found. However long it takes.

3789

Clara here. However long was too long. Ailan has joined Tanika in Immosa. May they both find the peace they were lacking in life.

Lissae is refusing to talk to me. She just chuckles every time I ask if there's a new Altoriae on the way.

Shael Robertson

Successes

Created the museum around Lissae's gateway.

Notes

3790

So that's why Lissae was laughing. Well met, Shael Robertson—our youngest Altoriae at four years old.

Also, Lissae. Four? Perhaps pick a warrior who is ready to fight, not still figuring out how to crawl.

No offence, Shael.

Patrols are increasing slightly. We have Lissaens out at least four nights a week. This doesn't seem like much of an increase, but pouring through the Handbook, it used to be two nights—three if it was busy.

Picking an Altoriae who has no concept of how to tie her shoes, let alone lead an army, is not something I would expect of our fair Realm, yet here we are.

Shael's training goes well. She picks things up quickly, but she remains a child and will be one for some time yet. I will not risk her before she is ready. No matter what sort of pressure the elders put on me.

The elders are insane. They've resorted to bribery to try to figure out who the Altoriae is. As if I'm just going to hand over her name.

I've sat down with the mayor this week and convinced him to draft duties for the townsfolk of Ronah. Of course, that includes the elders.

Such a shame they'll have to abide by it or leave Ronah.

As predicted, the elders were not impressed. Hopefully, they'll leave me alone to train the Altoriae without further inquiries.

Not quite as expected, but Ronah also wanted to have duties she upheld for the Altoriae, so I'm off to draft those.

3806

Welcome, Shael. It's time you had access to the biggest asset in your arsenal, The Altoriae's Handbook.

Clara, why in Lissae's green grass did you keep this from me? I've been the Altoriae for sixteen years.

Read it, Shael, and you'll understand.

While I appreciate the care Clara showed by not using the Handbook like a bedtime story, I do suggest that your Altoriae, dear Guardians, be allowed to access the book before they're twenty.

Unless, of course, they turn twenty before they become the Altoriae. Although that is looking less and less likely. The Realms remain much of a mystery to me, and patrolling is a foreign thing that others do and I have not been allowed to. It is difficult to lead others into battle when everyone else has had more experience.

I do not resent Clara, or her decision to keep me from these challenges, at all. I'm quite grateful that I had a relativity normal childhood.

Now, however, it's time to step up and lead my people.

After talking to the elders and the patrol members, the first thing that I want to change is the way patrols are run. It is unfair to expect the smallest population on Lissae to bear the weight of protecting the entire Realm.

There are plenty of Innarnians on the mainland and the fixed islands who can join our forces on a rotating basis. For the moment, they will need both training and integrating with the current groups, but within five years, they should be able to run their own groups and be assigned particular Realms to watch over.

Theoretically, having the same beings show up on the same Realm should help to encourage conversation, and hopefully lead to trust. How this goes in practice will be down to the patrol leader, and it will be interesting to see if it works.

I shall report back.

The mainlanders and Innarnians from the fixed islands have successfully integrated with our patrols. Training is going smoothly at the moment.

Clara is also on the hunt for an apprentice, and opening up to the other parts of Lissae means that she now has a much larger pool to choose from.

Mainlanders are jerks. Not all of them, of course, but one in particular. He seems to delight in pulling my braids and thinking it will endear him to me. We'll see how he likes a blade to the gut for his troubles.

The man has a death wish. He followed me home—after I stabbed him.

Are men normally like this?

No, he is rather...unique. Onto other news, shall I introduce my apprentice? Of course. Well met, apprentice.

Well met, Neev. May you walk the Realms with ease and your worst injury be a shallow paper cut.
My thanks, Altoriae, Guardian.

Apparently writing it means nothing. The mainlander who followed me home? He has quite a protective streak, which is mildly funny when I'm the one who ends up saving him.

Clara has put me on bed rest. I'm with child—not incapable!

3845

My daughter has arrived, and she is as perfect as her father.

To prevent bad tidings, I'll not mention either of their names here. Instead, I shall return to the mundane and inform you of the patrols.

Mainlanders have been patrolling regularly in their own groups. There have been only a few odd incidents, and mostly they are due to miscommunications. Those from the fixed islands are going well—better than their counterparts, at any rate.

I do worry though. It all seems to be running too smoothly.

3856

Trial and error has found that the patrols work well when there is a mix from across Lissae. It is still best for the same group to go out together. This way they can learn to work as a team, rather than as individuals with the same goal but different ways of achieving it.

I've been asked to attend a diplomatic party to Luerix. It's my first time off Lissae in years, and I must admit that I'm a tad excited.

The trip to Luerix went well. The standing stones around their gateway are amazing. We have nothing but forest around ours. I feel like that needs to change.

I've spoken to the elders, and they've agreed. As soon as the spring rains are over, the Earth Innarnians will construct a museum around our gateway. Give it a sense of grandeur, warded with confusion for those who aren't meant to be on Lissae, and a lesson for the patrol groups that ours is not the only Realm around. We must do our best to protect and preserve our neighbours and allies as well.

3859

The museum is finished! I'm so excited to see it finally open. The elders have asked me to say a few words, so I must away.

Crista Davis

Notes

Shael never returned. Neither did Clara. They were both crushed under a statue when the unveiling went horribly wrong.

Neav!

What am I meant to say, Crista?

Something less shocking?

My apologies. The Altoriae and her Guardian were in an accident. They did not survive.

Thank you.

I guess I'm the Altoriae now? Lissae spoke to me, like a whisper in the wind, right after Mum died.

I'd prefer to have her here, rather than talk to the Realm.

Uh, no offence.

Can Realms read?

Well met. I'm Crista Davis, 14. Tomorrow I'm meant to sit my exams, but the Lore Tellers are being weird and said they'd pass me 'because of what happened'.

Yay, no tests?

It feels like every thought is a question now, and most of them start with 'What if?'. Dad says it doesn't help.

I just wish Mum was still here.

Neav suggested I read the Handbook to get to know Mum better. She's something else. I'm glad I knew Neav before it... before.

I'm also glad Mum had me train. She didn't use the Handbook like a bedtime story (such a Mum thing to say), but she would tell me about the different Realms, and would quiz me on what plants would heal and which would harm and where to find them. I always thought it was a bit weird. You know, just one of the odd things that parents do when they pretend something is for your benefit.

From all her stories, I thought she went off-Realm loads, but not according to the Handbook. I guess she lived vicariously through Clara.

I can't believe Clara's gone too.

3860

Neev took me on patrol today. Dad was very not happy with her. Every other fifteen-year-old goes on patrol. How can I claim the title if I don't learn what to do?

It was tame, just checking gateways and getting used to the Portal. The Ducibus are unnerving, but Pala is lovely. Ze wished me a happy natal day and gave me a squishy not-cake thing. It was delicious.

3865

Patrols are standard now. The mainlanders are still playing nice, although you get the odd one or two every cycle who grumble until someone tells them to pull their heads in and they stop their muttering.

Neev has been teaching me how to use throwing knives. I still prefer a glaive, but the knives are a nice backup.

3867

Throwing knives are officially more than backup. They saved my life tonight. Patrolling Coqi, and I saw a swarm of spiders scurrying across the ground right towards me.

I threw a blade and watched the silver impale a spider, which kept moving, right through the blade. Coqi is the Realm that makes your nightmares come true. If you must visit, be aware, and don't believe anything you see.

3871

There are rumblings in the Dark Realms, and everyone seems on edge. Long-standing patrol groups have been split by senseless infighting, and I wonder if there's something in the air that's making so many beings act out of character.

Nope. I was wrong. They're just idiots.

    Crista!

    What? I'm right.

    What will the future Altoriaes think?

    That I tell the truth.

    ... Fair.

3873

The patrol groups have been reformed, which I find personally ridiculous, but if it means no one gets stabbed in the back, I guess I shouldn't complain.

    Someone got stabbed?

    Three someones, from four different groups (don't ask).

    ...?

    One was going out with two separate patrols. Turns out the others aren't super keen on that idea, so they decided to team up and stab the guy. He got one of them back. Then another, totally separate group decided to commit mutiny and abscond to Libertatia.

    The pirate Realm?

    That's the one.

    Where was I when this happened?

    At the trials, picking your apprentice.

    Ah, that explains it.

Introducing Aisling, my apprentice. She is a talented Innarnian, specialising in Crystal, Air, Earth, and Water.

Well met, Aisling. It's nice to see someone with multidisciplines.

Well met, Altoriae.

3876

There are more rumblings. The mainlanders are bringing complaints about Innarnian neighbours to Neav. It seems like a ploy to me, but I'm not sure what their end goal is.

3877

We thought they were mainlanders. They had been possessed by the Eni, and they were after Crista. One of them managed to slip past my guard, but one is all it takes, isn't it?

May you walk into Immosa and not need the knives strapped to your sides. And may the Eni who put you there rot in the bowels of whatever hell they fear the most.

Jali Thorne

Failures

On the evening after she announced who she was, her entire family was decimated bar her sister, Abby.

Killers

Accidentally trampled by a herd of Ullfin—a large rhinoceros-like beast with a scaly hide and long drooping ears.

Notes

Introducing Jali Thorne, tenth Attoriae. Read the Handbook and guard it with your life. It is your key to the Realms.

Well met, Aisling. I will aim to be a quick study.

I woke up with blood on my hands.

My parents and little brother, who I'd told my secret to just hours ago, lay across the room, sprawled at odd angles, strangled by their own intestines.

Flashes of memory—a voice, not my own, coming from my mouth, ordering them to stand in a line, Innarn pouring from my body, forcing them to comply. The shriek that left my father as he watched me rip my mother's guts from underneath skin and muscle. Hot, spurting blood hitting my face.

It was me, yet it wasn't. I was trapped in a cage, locked in the corner of my mind.

Thank Lissae that Abby was out with her friends.

And thank Aisling that she was able to snap me out of it.

Every time I am alone, I see a shadow out of the corner of my eye. I don't know what's happening, but it feels like I'm haunted.

We have spirits on Lissae, not ghosts, and they are usually friendly.

This one feels the opposite of friendly.

Jali was, in fact, seeing a Shadow Bringer. And it was not friendly. I am so sorry I didn't take you more seriously. I will do better by your sister.

Abby Thorne

Notes

3880

Introducing Jali's sister, Abby Thorne, as the eleventh Attoriae.

You failed my sister. I will not let you do the same to me.

I never meant to fail her. I swear on Lissae that I will put your life before my own, always.

We shall see.

It's about time that I introduced my apprentice as well. Tabatha hails from Goudnotia, and is talented in Healing, Water, Air and Soul Innaru.

Well met, Guardian.

Read and remember. This book will be your key to understanding the Realms.

Aisling has stepped into Immosa, thanks to a fireball that was meant for me. I hate that she lived up to her promise, but I am thankful for it.

Sometimes I see shadows that should not be there, dancing on the walls.

Puppet masters with no one pulling the strings, they make me smile every time.

The peace and sense of being that I feel when I go to investigate these shadows defies anything I can believe. It's like the peace and love from those passed flows from them straight into me when they are near.

Tabatha is worried about the shadows on the wall, especially considering what happened to Jali.

It's a valid concern.
Jali never spoke about a peaceful feeling when it happened.

Still valid.

3938

Decades of patrols, and countless arguments solved. Is this all the Altoriae is? I can remember being so jealous when Jali was named. Now, I have no idea why. I suppose the water is always clearer on someone else's beach.

3942

Activity is ramping up in the Light Realms again. Honestly, they think they're subtle, but it's like being smacked with a brick to the face. You absolutely know you're hit.

3958

When one side of the Portal calms down, the other arcs up. Now the Dark Realms are being sly and savage, much like a shem'ar who wants the last bit of your toast—they'll bite your ankle just to get a snack.

Did Pippin bite you again?
Besides the point.
I'm not entirely sure that beast is a shem'ar.
Me either. Pretty sure he's part dragon, or dinosaur, or something.

3960

Ulnan is no more. Reports say that the O'Aralide army descended upon the Realm and burned everything to the ground. There is one survivor, a healer who fled to Lissae, and I was not about to deny her entry.

Beware the O'Aralide who comes calling, lest Lissae fall in the same way Ulnan did.

3971

The O'Aralide did come calling, but that's not what got Abby. Something that looked and sounded like me lured her to a safe spot and slit her throat while her back was turned.

May she step into Immosa knowing I would never betray her.

Fiona MacAde

Notes

3972

I am old. The search for an apprentice feels never-ending.

3974

Well met, Resa Sunab, apprentice and soon to be Guardian.

Well met, Guardian. I have much to learn before I could possibly take on your role.

Learn fast, Resa. I am so very tired.

3981

Lissae has announced her new Attoriae.

Well met, Fiona MacAde, twelfth Attoriae.

Well met, Guardian Tabatha and Apprentice Resa.

Well met, Attoriae.

3982

I had the privilege of knowing Tabatha for only a year, and she taught me so much. May Immosa grant her the rest she has been seeking.

Sometimes, I have flashes of memory that remind me the past Altoriaes are always with me. Today, I was walking through ruins on Crihimos. I could taste the tang of a long-gone ocean in the air, feel the sand beneath my feet instead of the soil, feel heat on my skin instead of the bitter cold of winter. I wonder who visited Crihimos when the town a day's walk from the gateway was in its prime? It must have been beautiful. What happened to it? Was it just time? The retreat of the ocean? I've scoured the Handbook, and the diaries too, and there is no mention of it anywhere. Another mystery lost to the ages.

The spirits seem exceptionally active lately. I wonder if there is something happening in their Realm which I'm not privy to? They do not like to talk about it, no matter how nicely I ask.

Something is happening on the Realms. There's talk of a split within some of the Light Realms, and every time I enter the Portal, another army is on the move.

I know there is a perception that the Dark Realms are fiercer, but I find the opposite true. Many from the Light Realms will smile to your face and stab you as soon as your back is turned. The beings from the Dark Realms will happily look into your eyes as they kill you. I suppose, for most of them, there's little point to the pretences the Light Realms indulge in.

I'm so glad Resa survived. Who walks into a pack of metsari and pokes them?! And who thinks licking poisonous spit is a good idea? I swear to Lissae, my Guardian will be the death of me.

And no, you stupid book, I don't believe in the curse, so you can shove that thought up your spine and smile.

Wait. Can books smile?

If you break the spine in the right way.

Resa! Book spines are not meant to bend that way.

You asked.

My Guardian is a menace

And you love it.

I would very much like the Light Realms to go back to fighting amongst themselves and stop trying to invade Lissae, pretty please.

And now the Grey Realms are joining in. They can all go jump in a boiling acid pool somewhere.

Pretty sure some of them would enjoy that.

Blerg.

Of course, the others stop, so the Dark Realms figure it's their turn. Can't they all just forget to get out of bed or something?

Wishful thinking.

3995

Fiona MacAde stepped in front of a scythe and took the hit for me.

It's meant to be the other way around.

I'll miss you, my Altoriae. May Immosa greet you with open arms.

3996

Introducing Joshua, my apprentice.

Well met, Guardian.

It is our job to keep Lissae safe until she names her next Attoriae, however long that takes.

I will serve with honour.

4001

Resa was able to teach me enough to survive, and the book should do the rest. The Attoriae has yet to make herself known, so I will continue to protect Lissae as Resa directed.

The first thing I must do is find an apprentice. Resa would have…

It's my fault, you know? That Resa died. She was tired, wanted to leave the patrol up to me, but I said I wasn't ready.

Guess I don't have a choice about it now.

Ready or not, Lissae, I'm your protector until you announce the next Attoriae.

4029

Is everyone incompetent, or am I just unlucky? Two apprentices down, and another is ready to step into their place. Here's hoping she lasts long enough to see the Handbook.

4036

Nope. The search continues, as do the relentless, daily patrols.

4040

Another three—dead. I'm losing faith that Lissae knows what she's doing.

A scrap of a boy washed up on the shore today, with colours as bright as mine. Perhaps he's a sign.

Or an idiot. Tried to fireball his own throat. Who does that?

He arrived on a battlefield, with no knowledge of how he got there. Me thinks the Realm is playing games. I'm just not sure who she wants to win, and what it will cost the loser.

He found the book. I guess that means Lissae is done playing, and we were just waiting for the right being. Introducing Jonathan Suan, ship's boy turned apprentice.

Well met, Guardian.

4045

Joshua sacrificed himself to ensure that I would make it home. I can only hope that I live to meet my Altoriae. May he walk the halls of Immosa alongside the family he gave everything for.

Shari Dawn

Successes

~~Defeat of Anriluka~~ *Didn't feel like much of a defeat.*

Founding the Altoriae's Guild

Visions

Tania Hollingsworth fighting by her side against the hantra in Ronah's graveyard.

Alliances

Anthea, a Joratre of Vutolea

Jerran, U'sala leader of 4059

Yessna, U'sala leader of

Ebb of Gerhar (Potential ally)

Prime Lakin of Tocithas

Notes

4053

I have met the Altoriae.

Many times, actually. A slip of a girl who has been masquerading as a Blank in order to protect her family. What sort of child should carry a burden like that?

She doesn't know about the book yet. Barely wants to know me. I have spent so many years wondering what it would be like to meet my Altoriae that I never once imagined she would want nothing to do with me.

Still, when you get to read this, well met, Shari Dawn, thirteenth Altoriae. You are stronger than you know, more than anyone else sees

4055

Introducing Mitchel Hoffman, my apprentice.

Well met, Guardian.
May your time as an apprentice be long and fulfilling.

4056

Well met, Guardian Buan.

What, exactly, am I meant to write in the book?
Whatever you think will help the next Altoriae, Shari.

What if there isn't a next one?
Lissae will continue. I promise.

Not what I asked, Jon.

It seems like an impossible task, saving the world every day. I am finding it entirely possible, just exceptionally tiring.

The hard part of this calling—if you wish to call it that—is that it is soul-crushing and mind-numbingly repetitive. It's always the same old story—bad guy tries to take over the Realm, I shove them back into theirs. Why don't the bad guys help save our Realm for once, instead of trying to take it over? There are worse things I could wish for, aren't there?

4059

Introducing Samuel, my apprentice.

Well met.

May your time as

Oh, no you don't. I've heard about this book. You can stop right there. Samuel, it's nothing to worry about. Would you worry more with my teeth around your throat? Fine.

It's official. I have my own guild. I asked and checked, and they still want to join in the fight to protect Lissae. They pledged:

We swear to protect Lissae and do everything in our power to keep our Realm safe. We will fight by the Altoriae's side and guard each other's backs no matter where we are.

But I made a pledge too. I swore to do everything in my power to keep them and Lissae safe.

And I will uphold the pledge.

During the fight against the Crystal Intelligence, I died. My atoms and essence scattered across the Realm, but Lissae brought me back together again.

My memory of being dead is fading, but I know I saw two hearts that day. And only one was shattered.

Lissae warned me of something. Crossing a portal? The words have faded, but the way she sent them hasn't.

Something is going on with my Realm.

And I intend to find out what.

I failed my pledge. Amara died, and I wasn't there to stop it.

What else could go wrong?

That is not something you should write in this book.

What else could go wrong?

Shari!

He stole the book. The waste of flesh and breath stole the Handbook and ripped it to shreds. I've been working on restoring it, but I fear some of the pages were lost. You'll have to make do, little protector, and add what is missing to the book, should you find it.

GUARDIANS

Welcome to the most challenging task of your life:

Keeping your Altoriae alive.

Guardian is the rank of the person who is in charge of training and caring for the Altoriae, and for Lissae. In cases of emergency, the mayor and elders defer to the Guardian.

Should the Altoriae fall, or be unable to fulfil her duties, it is up to you. Would that such a thing never happens.

If Kay'imi is anything to go by, your Altoriae will be stubborn, fierce, and determined that nothing will stop her. She will most likely work herself into an early grave if she doesn't receive the rest she requires. She will reach Immosa even sooner if she doesn't stop reading over my shoulder while I write.

I find the Altoriae is someone who Lissae depends on almost entirely for protection. This is not sustainable. It is up to you, Guardian, to make sure that your Altoriae has someone to rely on. Never let them down, and don't let them fail.

That is your ongoing task, should you be up to the challenge.

If you are not, walk away now. This life is not for you.

— *Met'sara.*

LIST OF GUARDIANS

Met'sara

Eminlith

Azulie Von Dayme

Thuk

Qar

Ullmar

Estebar

Liadain

Ailan

Clara

Neev

Aisling

Tabatha

Resa Sunab

Joshua Clemise

Jonathan Suan

Mitchel Hoffman

Samuel Caragnton

Duties

First and Foremost:	Protecting the Altoriae
Secondly:	Teaching the Altoriae
Thirdly:	Keeping the Altoriae's identity a secret
Fourthly:	Calling Ronah's residents to arms in times of need
Fifthly:	Teaching Ronah's residents
Sixthly:	Maintaining peace on Lissae
Seventhly:	Ensuring Lissae's young remember their elders' pledges to the Altoriae
And Eighthly:	Maintaining *The Altoriae's Handbook* for the use of future Altoriaes

Secrecy

The Altoriae must not be revealed before she is ready to take her test.

That's it. Do not tell a soul until she's ready.

How much clearer can I be? Tell no one.

Instinct

Sometimes you will wonder if you are doing the right thing, particularly when you do not know who the Altoriae is. During these times, Lissae will guide you.

If there is one thing the Realm has told us, it's that we will know when we are in the presence of our Altoriae. All that needs to occur is that we meet her eyes. As soon as that connection happens, everything will fall into place. Your instincts will drive you to your knees before her, and she will bow to you.

If she does not bow, then she is not the true Altoriae. While that hasn't happened before, it is worth noting. Even injured, tortured, or in screaming pain, she will still bow.

APPRENTICES

The Guardian's Apprentice traditionally undergoes testing in order to be chosen. This is made up of three trials. The apprentice must undertake intensive training to ensure the safety of the Altoriae. The Guardian's Apprentice is to take over the role of Guardian once the current holder of the title falls in battle or dies of old age.

The duties of an apprentice are much the same as their Guardian and mentor, with the addition of being ready to step into the role of Guardian as soon as the one before them falls, assuming apprentices make it that far.

List of fallen apprentices

Cal'vie

She'far

Xantus

Melforae

Khia'des

Oriyran

Zin'rorah

Lau'arin

Francis Hobbs

Bianca Thorne

Sheriadan Malloy

Ayeisha Clemments

Brandon Yarrow

Aruli Ribeck

Lonnah Thorne

Kalleria Dawn

Thalice Silverstone

Mitchel Hoffman

ORACLES, PROPHESIES & FOREWARNINGS

From the Darkness comes the saviour of Grey.

The Mother Realm will provide again.

The fate of the new depends on the change of Gold:

Dark or Grey? Walk through, or let the Mother pass?

    - made by Istaniern of the Q'Aralide

Linked by blood, the Guardian's Dark relative

Will be the saviour or downfall of Lissae's child.

The invitation cannot be revoked,

Unless Lissaen blood is spilled.

At the final hour, he must choose to die

Or to conquer.

The fate of the child lies with him.

    - from *Guardian*

(The Light hiding in the deep) seeks you, and we fear it won't rest until you are no more.

    - made by Prime Lakin

Start the curse

Through all the True

Come a being

Dark from agony

Under the angry galaxy

Silence fills the night

Slow to all

Come a bright new death

Until an Altoriae

Find a thorn red jewel

And free the cure

From the shining (life force–blood?)

Of Anriluka

Ten by day.

    - From Ronah

You must know, dear one, that one of your guild is not who they claim to be. The one who you have doubted all along. You set sights on him and decided him to be false. He refuses to tell you his proper name yet flaunts his power to others when you are not around, hoping to keep them in check using their fear of his kind.

He feels more freedom than he has ever experienced before... I believe the changeling is true to you.

It is our wish that you are not the one to do the unthinkable. If you are, his reign will destroy our Realms and the surrounding ones. If you are to die when he is watching, so shall we all.

    - made by Zana

LISSAE

Our home is a Grey, sentient Realm on the second band. She relies on you, Altoriae, to defend her.

Comprised of six continents, seven sentient Shifting Islands and multiple fixed islands, she is home to ten races.

Lissae is said to be a Mother Realm. There are two moons in her orbit.

Outside of the Shifting Islands, Innarnians are becoming endangered. Hatred towards those who have a power they cannot control is growing, and I fear what will happen when it overflows.

—Jonathan Brian 4058

Lissae is more than a Realm. She guides and guards her people through the Altoriae, and her Guardian. When one of us falls, it is up to Lissae to pick the next being to protect her from everyone who wants to take over her lands and her beings. It might not be what you expect, but having held the title for most of my life, I dearly hope it is not passed on to you, reader.

—Shari Dawn, 4059

GEOGRAPHY AND COSMOLOGY

Mainland

Dento

Innovation and progress come slow to Dento, as its permanent residents, the Kumaru, are long lived.

Capital city
Earthwall

Built at the base of a mountain using advanced Earth construction techniques, the capital city sees beings of all types pass through its gates.

Townships

Demis Vale	Rosemore	Munrath Wood
Ebonwick	Granit Hill	North Basalt

Main population
Kumaru

Tree-like humanoids from Lissae. They are usually found on Dento and are high-level Earth Innarnians. They pride themselves on their connection with Earth and Spirit Innarn. A long-lived race, they rarely step off-Realm.

Important places/buildings
The forests are the most important places in Dento, as they contain the lifeblood that ensures the Kumaru ancestors will continue.

Trade goods

Minerals	Gemstones	Plants

Gondnotia

The bottom part of Gondnotia was created to be a refuge for those who had to flee their own Realms and were forced to resettle somewhere new.

Capital city
Pliapeak

Situated on the top of a hill in the middle of a heavily guarded forest, Pliapeak is where you can find everything from buildings that scrape the sky to shacks on the outskirts.

Townships

Bralloth Hill	Lower Thragstaff	Subban Heights
Brilun Woods	Scirton Valley	Upper Nerul

Main population
Diaxampal

Refugees from the Grey Realm of **Daixam**, now living on Lissae.

Greonilae

Refugees from the Grey Realm of Greon, now living on Lissae.

Humans

Like many places on Lissae, Humans make up the main population.

Ofanahni

Native to Bazaven, the Ofanahni are typically oppressed by the Sylpans, whose brutal and inconsistent justice system makes their lives difficult. A group of Ofanahni refugees has settled in the desert region of the continent set aside on Lissae for refugees.

Sivote

Refugees from the Grey Realm of **Riomache**, now living on Lissae.

Teeldrit

A small, friendly population of Teeldrit refugees live in the desert region of the continent set aside on Lissae for refugees.

Vladine

Refugees from the Grey Realm of **Vinneča**, now living on Lissae.

Important places/buildings

Gondnotia's museum is a wonder to behold. It contains artefacts not just from Lissae, but from the Realms of the refugees as well. Without the museum, much of the history of Lissae's newest settlers would be lost within generations.

A small, but dedicated team ensures this doesn't happen. They focus not just on items and written history, but verbal storytelling as well, inviting elders from the new settlers to come and share their history.

Trade goods

Glass　　　　　　　　Salt　　　　　　　　Reed

Kenorvia

Housing mostly non-Innarnians, those from Kenorvia tend to bite first and ask questions later.

Capital city
Freyford

The city was built on the banks of a carefully crafted harbour. Its allure is matched by the backdrop of majestic forests.

Townships

Highmere	Bearmond	Westhallow
Stagmond	Littlegrove	Fairforest

Main population
Human

Important places/buildings
Blacksmiths

Every town in Kenorvia has schools, shops, and homes, but the most important place is always the blacksmiths. Across the nation, different smithies specialise in various items, but each one is essential.

Trade goods

Timber	Jewellery	Silver

Lawrgaea

From the icy north to the temperate south, Lawrgaea is home to a mostly non-Innarnian population.

Capital city
Highvault

Deep in the Vauntus Mountains, the capital of Lawrgaea sits between sheets of ice and walls of rock.

Townships

Vineux	Béluçon	Alenseau
Colcourt	Aubersir	Montauçon

Main population
Human

Da'mar

A humanoid race with lizard-like features who reside in subterranean dwellings–doorways to which can be found in the most obscure places. They lived by a warrior code that is difficult for other races to understand. It is speculated that most of their doorways are on Lawrgaea, but no one from the surface can really be sure.

Important places/buildings
Spice Markets

While Lawrgaeans value their meat, this is the place where they truly come to life. Beings from all over Lissae come to haggle for the best spices on the Realm, which can only ever be found in a Lawrgaean spice market.

Trade goods

Bricks	Spices	Meat

Nelonia

Bound in snow and ice, Nelonia is the coldest continent on Lissae. The beings there are usually of stout build and have adapted to their chilly climate.

Capital city
Veernia

Found at the northernmost tip of Nelonia, the capital is a fortress built from ever-lasting ice bricks.

Townships

Gyfþustr	Begþir	Másvaldeidr
Állandátr	Ýd	Fygr

Main population
Human

Important places/buildings
Peaskspire Pass

A gap in the mountain range between Veernia in the north and Ýd on the east coast, everyone works to keep it clear so trade can be facilitated across the continent. Veernia finds it easier to trade with Kenorvia to the west, while Ýd trades with Hulios and Dento to the east, and Freeson and Gondnotia to the north.

Trade goods

Flax	Wine	Cloth

Rohinda

One of the largest continents, Rohinda is home to Innarnians and non-Innarnians alike. The most temperate of the mainlands, it's perfect for grazing and growing crops that don't survive in colder climates.

Capital city
Nimea

Placed at the end of the river that divides Rohinda, Nimea comprises green spiralling towers and glittering windows.

Townships

Kleia	Evodine	Monithei
Arasine	Phaethus	Seriphoia

Main population
Humans

Important places/buildings
Euthemillia River

Running from the north to the south, the river cuts through the middle of Rohinda and is the perfect way to get goods to Nimea.

Farmland

If threatened, every Rohindan will drop what they're doing to save the farmlands. They are more than a source of trade; they are the livelihood and life of many of the beings who call Rohinda home.

Trade goods

Wool	Lead	Fruit

Vendalbara

A place where ocean meets land in perfect synergy, Vendalbara is home to mostly hard-working non-Innarnians who live off the goods of the sea, the mountains, or the forests.

Capital city
Freehorne

Guardian Buan's hometown.

Townships

Rockshade	Sunford	Bayview
Edgegrasp	Glimmermire	Goldshear

Main population
Human

Important places/buildings
The Docks

As a country which relies on goods sought from water, places that allow access are seen as a priority for upkeep. The docks across Vendalbara are kept as immaculate as possible.

Steepshire Ranges

The mountain range that rings the northern part of Vendalbara

Trade goods

Deep-sea Fish	Cosmo shell	Gold

Fixed Islands

Freeson

A long island that sits beside the coast of Gondnotia, Freeson has three towns for its mostly human population.

Townships

Gardid   Cragnet   Baothad

Important places/buildings
The Three Crags

Three dormant volcanoes dot Freeson and are home to all sorts of vegetation that, when crushed, produce the most amazing dyes.

Trade goods

Dyes   Chemicals   Garments

Hulios

Found at the bottom of Dento, Hulios is a tiny dot of land that broke away when the refugee land was added to Gondnotia. Despite its small size, the island houses over a thousand beings who live, work, and play within the walls of the only city.

Important places/buildings
The City

Sitting between mountain walls to the north and south, the town of Hulios is simply referred to as "the city".

Trade goods

Tea   Rice   Furniture

Jinkor

Placed below Kenorvia and above Muhara, Jinkor is home to innovation and exploration. Their human population lives in six towns and has the largest naval fleet on Lissae.

Townships

Bastilion	Dewmore	Hillside
Bayeful	Busterdale	Ferngrove

Important places/buildings
Bayeful harbour

Home of Jinkor's steamship fleet.

Trade goods

Toslzura beans	Livestock	Steamships

Muhara

Southwest of Jinkor, Muhara is a small island with big ambitions. Home to a human population contained in one icy town, Muhara is known for its vallen herd beasts, which can be bred for fur, meat, and cheese.

Important places/buildings

Mostly flat, the plains of Muhara are carefully guarded. Vallens may produce all their trade goods, but they aren't particularly bright and have been known to wander unimpeded into icy water and simply forget to return to land.

Trade goods

Furs	Vallen meat	Cheese

Nindonia

East of Lawrgaea, Nindonia rings a large hot spring. Houses crop up where there is clear land. Although they will tell outsiders that their capital is the small village on the southern tip, they count the whole island as one city.

Main population
Zindara

A race of humanoids. They are high-level Plasma and Fire Innarnians.

Important places/buildings
The walled fortress in the north contains their schools and the training grounds for the prized Nindonian messenger birds.

Trade goods

Seeds	Birds	Bamboo

Omina

The second smallest of the fixed islands, Omina sits east of Lawrgaea and south of Nindonia, big enough for only one city of humans.

Important places/buildings
Felagave

The forest that houses the gilagoats.

Trade goods

Ziom	Tack	Beasts of burden

Opestila

Neighbouring Vendalbara and Sulanta, it has long been thought that this small fixed island was once an ice drift that an Innarnian chose to build on. Although it is larger than Tevon, less than one hundred humans call it home.

Important places/buildings
Anywhere warm.

Trade goods

Instruments   Scribe equipment   Tools

Sulanta

Found in the very north of Lissae, between Opestila and Lawrgaea, the forges of Sulanta's four towns keep the island from freezing over.

Townships
Snowvale   Windsigh   Crispendale
Hearthdrom

Main population
Uleulan

A race of four-armed humanoids from Lissae. Usually found on Sulanta, they have distinct features: a single, large eye and translucent skin. They includee some of the Realm's high-level Water and Spirit Innarnians.

Trade goods
Cosmetics   Artwork   Armour

Tevon

Situated between Vendalbara and Rohinda, Tevon is one of the smallest fixed islands of Lissae. It has a population of only a few hundred humans.

Trade goods

Weapons   Ondirhund hair   Oil

Creatures
Giggler

A risus bird. Healed by Lira after her young brother gave her the injured bird. Twice as large as a regular risus, Giggler had black plumage and a deep-throated laugh which terrified anyone who heard it.

Vutana

Sitting between Kenorvia on the west and Gondnotia on the east, Vutana is perfectly positioned for trade.

Capital city
The island is small enough to have just one township of humans and satyrs.

Important places/buildings
Hemibise shoals

Found along the banks of the island, the glowing stones rest amongst the seagrass if one knows where to look.

Trade goods

Hemibise   Medical machinery   Ink

Yaston

A small island off the coast of Rohinda, Yaston is home to around three thousand humans and the infamous Sephina Ranges.

Capital city
Castaria

Nestled against the Sephina Ranges, the town boasts white walls against the green hills, making for a striking contrast. One of the older capitals, Castaria has survived sieges, plagues, and on one memorable occasion the water in their wells turning to whisky thanks to an Innarn prank gone wrong.

Important places/buildings
Sephina Ranges

Home of the Darfionious Oak tree, these ranges ensure the production of sephina silk, a major trading good.

Trade goods
   Darfionious Oaks   Sephina silk

Shifting Islands

The name for the group of islands that travel around Lissae's seas, seemingly on a whim. They are sentient beings who care for the residents who make them their home.

Unique features

Buildings

Bereni trees

Trees that are grown to be used as buildings. The size and design of the tree can be controlled by an Innarnian or by one of the sentient islands.

Rezem

A building built out of a mound of earth. The size and design of the mound can be controlled by an Innarnian or by one of the sentient islands.

People

Clans

Family lines.

Elders

Those who have, through age and experience, managed to survive the Realms long enough to guide their people. They also act as advisors to the mayor.

Linked

A soul joined with that of one of Lissae's Shifting Islands. As the Shifting Islands are sentient, it was decided long ago that they should link with a being on their Island to ensure that they remain in touch with the current needs of their population, and not remove themselves from the trials and tribulations of everyday beings.

Lore Keeper

The eldest of the Wisara is given the title of Lore Keeper and charged with passing down the tales of Lissae to those on the Shifting Islands. This is typically done as payment and called the Tales of Lore.

Lore Teller

An oral storyteller who passes on information from previous generations. They are held in high regard by the general population and are thought to be unable to lie.

Returned

The name given to those from Ronah who survived being eaten by Anriluka.

328 years ago, Anriluka decimated the population of Ronah, eating 2761 people of the 3042 population, leaving 281 people alive.

Of the 2761 people who are now amongst the Returned:

497	under 14 years old
366	between 15 - 24 years old
1680	between 25 - 100 years old
218	100 + years old

Of the people who returned, 2198 survived the ensuing fight with the rest of Anriluka's meals, leaving:

282	under 14 years old
304	between 15 - 24 years old
1478	between 25 - 100 years old
134	100 + years old

Out of the 2198 people, there are 246 family groups and 302 unattached people. Of the unattached, there are 56 under 14 years old. Out of the 2198 people, 119 decided to move to the mainland (3 family groups and 116 unattached people).

This leaves 243 family groups and 130 unattached people that Ronah must build houses for. 66 of the unattached people have decided to live together in 16 groups.

Ronah must build houses for 16 groups, 64 singles, and 243 family groups, bringing the total of the to-be-constructed buildings to 323.

Ronah can produce approximately 10 Bereni or Rezem per week. An architectural Innarnian can produce 2 houses per week alone. There are 26 architectural Innarnian in the Returned. Together, they can produce 60 buildings per week.

Technomancer

The head of the Techno Centre has been given the nickname of technomancer due to the number of times her advances have brought the seemingly deceased back to life.

Akoren

One of the sentient Shifting Islands on Lissae. Originally home to Lissae's deities, she is inhabited by the **Wisara** and refugees from the mainland who required a place to stay after the civil war.

Capital city
Merthin

Akoren's main city is underwater. Home to the **Wisara**.

Townships
Fog City

Found in Akoren, this city is the highest point of all the Shifting Islands. It sits within the clouds. There is a tale about how the first Ilutri flew through the fog at the top of the mountain and crashed into it. After the accident, they decided to make the peak their home.

Osithys

Known as the rainy plane city, this is where most of the refugees have settled on **Akoren**.

Main population
Wisara

Primarily ocean-dwelling beings whose bodies, although humanoid, look like the tangled roots of lotus flowers. Their 'hair' is the leaves of the lotus, and the flowers act as adornments. Wisara can change form to a more traditional humanoid shape and inhabit land areas in either form. They move around as travellers and trade between the continents and islands of Lissae by walking the ocean beds. They are the perfect oversea (or in this case, undersea) merchants, as storms have little to no effect on them. Custom dictates that the Wisara are offered fish and bread and other items to restock their larder by the towns they visit. As payment, the Wisara will tell the Tales of Lore.

Only the eldest of the Wisara is given the title of **Lore Keeper**, although anyone could tell the tales.

Schools

Schooling for the Wisara is mostly informal, with lessons taught as play happens.

Important places/buildings
Wandering Serpent, The

A tavern in **Merthin**, favoured by **Domic Iabor** and **Brayden**.

Trade goods

Traders by nature, the Wisara make their living by shipping goods and information all over Lissae.

Current Linked
Domic Iabor

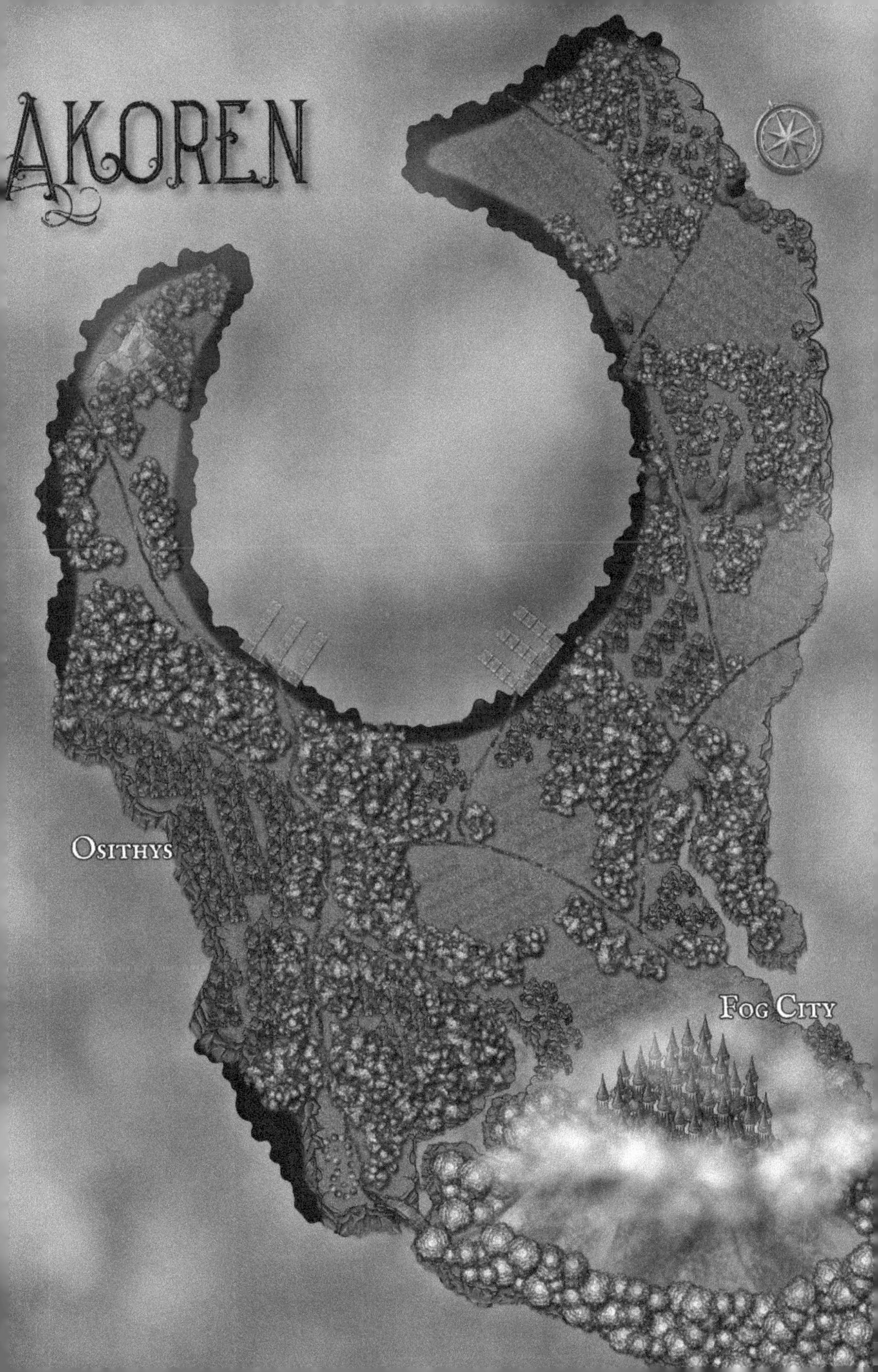

Akoren

Cantash

One of the sentient Shifting Islands on Lissae, he is home to the Daens. The Shifting Island has a ridge of mountains running around the circumference, with one side of the island home to active volcanoes.

Capital city

Cantash, like Ronah, only has the one city base. Above ground, the Daens live and play, while underground they learn, farm, and work.

Main population
Daen

A short, fierce, and loyal race with amazing control over the Fire Element.

Schools

There are four schools on Cantash that sit on the main compass points. Each has a door to get to and from the other quickly, in case of emergency, or during a prank war.

Tradition dictates that in the last week of the school year, a prank war is called. It's the perfect way for students to let off steam after exams. During the prank war, there are three rules: nothing permanent, nothing harmful, and don't get caught.

Ignis Academy

One of the schools on **Cantash**. Ignis Academy caters to older teens.

Important places/buildings
Cantash's Museum

Two charcoal black doors with a welcome sign greet visitors to the museum.

Gardens

Being an island of fire, it was long ago decided to protect Cantash's produce by putting it underground. The gardens are home to most of Cantash's creatures and are ringed by schools, businesses, workshops, farms and more. Often referred to as "green time".

The Lift

Set into the side of a cliff are two massive, steel double doors that guard the biggest secret on **Cantash**–the **Gardens**. The Lift is accessible only to Innarnians. Stepping through the doors, you enter a giant metal box that can take you down to the **Gardens**.

Trade goods

Calromata   Eobustus

Current Linked
Fenix

GANTASH

Ginorti

One of the sentient Shifting Islands on Lissae. He is home to the Satyrs. Filled with forests and rolling hills, Ginorti is the perfect spot for a siege, especially when you can't be sure which of the trees are ancient Kumaru.

Capital city
Much like Cantash and Ronah, Ginorti has only one area where beings live, the rest is forest or farmland.

Main population
Kumaru

Tree-like humanoids from Lissae. They originated on Ginorti before moving to Dento.

Satyrs

A humanoid race with legs and a tail similar to that of a horse from Lissae. They are usually found on Ginorti. They include some of the finest crack troops on the Realm.

School
Briar's Hall

Schooling focuses mostly on weapons and offensive/defensive Innarn.

Trade goods
Sand pears   Persea

Current Linked
Oakley

Rakemyst

One of the sentient Shifting Islands on Lissae. He is home to the Ilutri. Dotted with floating Islands that contain everything from wildlife to extensive estates, Rakemyst can prove difficult for Blanks and those without Air Innarn to get around.

Capital city

Like the other Shifting Islands, Rakemyst does not have a capital.

Main population

Ilutri

Winged humanoids from Lissae. They are usually found on Rakemyst and are high-level Innarnians. They include some of the finest archers on the Realm.

Schools

Thistlewood Institute

The school on Rakemyst.

Important places/buildings

The Head of the Elders lives on their own separate floating island. Not only does this homestead hold the dwelling for the Head Elder's family, but also includes extensive gardens.

The Tower

In the centre of Rakemyst, the tower is a place of culture and learning.

Trade goods

Aerial protection   Feathers

Current Linked

Zana

N
RAKEMYST

Ronah

One of the sentient Shifting Islands on Lissae. Ronah is one of the six gateways to the Realms. *She's alright, for a hunk of sentient dirt.*

Crying islands are potentially more annoying than crying beings.

Capital city

Ronah is small enough that there is only one township on the island.

Main population

Ronah is home to a variety of races and the traditional home of the Altoriae.

Schools
Ridden Hall

The school on Ronah.

Important places/buildings
Books 'n' More

A store on Ronah that Guardian Buan runs when he's not saving the Realm of Lissae.

Castle, Ronah's

The centre point of Ronah and the traditional home of the Altoriae, the Guardian, and their respective families. The base of it was made from a huge volcanic crater, one that had ceased its activity on Kay'imi's command. This left incredible natural catacombs beneath the castle that were mostly used for storage or the occasional prison cell. Merged with the top of the crater is a wall of plasma, complete with a doorknocker that booms every time it is used. Windows of clear air dot the structure, and those inside can choose to darken or lighten them at will. A bereni tree grew at the heart of the castle, making not only a secure place for the Altoriae to train, but a solid structure should the outer walls fail. The branches and leaves of the tree make up the majority of the rest of the castle, except for the top, which sprouts turrets of flame, and the surface of the second floor, which is made of blue-green water. Formally known as Castle Bachelor.

Healers Centre

Also called the Hospital. A place to go when sick or injured.

Quiver and Quill Tavern, The

The tavern run by the thirteenth Altoriae's parents.

Trade goods

Fish   Off-Realm protection

Current Linked
Tania Hollingsworth

Townsfolk

Due to Ronah's housing of the Altoriae, a list of current residents must be kept up to date at all times. This is to ensure that:

- There are no interlopers (from off or on-Realm)
- Accurate records are maintained

During times of conflict, it is acceptable to update after the final skirmish is over.

These pages are missing from the Handbook entirely I wonder if the scum of Lissae who decided to steal the book put them somewhere, and if so, how did he know to take these pages?

N
BEACH STREET
BEACH STREET
SUMMER CLOSE
RIDDEN ROAD
LITTORAL DRIVE
BARKLEY STREET
CALLOWAY STREET
DEW DRIVE
SHORT STREET
CALLOWAY STREET
ARROW STREET
BARKLEY STREET
RIDDEN ROAD
WINNER ROAD
LITTORAL ROAD
Castle Bachelor
Tania's house
SPRING STREET
Jonathan's house
Shari's house
WEAVER DRIVE
WEAVER DRIVE
WEAVER DRIVE
RIDDEN ROAD
FERN ROAD
AUTUMN DRIVE
RIDDEN ROAD
BARKLEY STREET
ASTRAL ROAD
BEACH STREET
METTA STREET
Ridden Hall
ASTRAL ROAD
IRONY WAY
RIDDEN ROAD
BEACH STREET
RONAH

Talhan

One of the sentient Shifting Islands on Lissae, and the only one to start with an all-human population. He now accepts immigrants across Lissae.

Capital city
Crystal Province

Home of the Techno Centre and innovation, this is where you want to be.

Unless it's overrun by Atlantian machines fuelled by Femto-crystals—then you want to be far, far away

Townships

Earth Province	Fire Province	Old Province
Plasma Province	Water Province	

Main population
Home to beings from all over Lissae, Talhan welcomes those from off-Realm as well. Two of Talhan's most famous residents—the technomancers—are not of Lissaen origin.

Ulnanian

A race from Ulnan. The only known surviving member is Temira, one of the technomancers.

Schools
Vitreus Academy

The school on Talhan. Vren is the current head of the academy.

Important places/buildings
Healing Centre

Talhan's version of the Healers Centre. The building also holds the **Techno Centre**, and the labs of the technomancers and Talhan's Linked.

The Heart of Talhan

Hidden within the most protected layers, the Heart of Talhan is usually only accessible by Talhan's Linked. Recently, I was able to glimpse the heart. The drawing does not do it justice.

Techno Centre

Located on Talhan, it is the hub for all of Lissae's crystal and technological advances. The dual heads of the Techno Centre have been given the nickname of the technomancers, due to the amount of times their advances have brought the seemingly deceased back to life. The building also holds the Healing Centre, and the labs of the technomancers and Talhan's Linked.

Trade goods

Medicinal goods   Semi-sentient crystal

Current Linked

Cyrus Petram

N

Talha

Farm Land

Water
Province

Earth
Province

Fire
Province

Plasma
Province

Spirit
Province

Crystal
Province

Air
Province

Vannali

One of the sentient Shifting Islands on Lissae. She is home to both myth and Weavers.

Capital city

Vannali is another of the Shifting Islands without a capital.

Main population

Weavers

A strong Innarnian race, they reside on Vannali and usually keep to themselves. They are regarded as one of the oldest races and are often considered mythical beings as they rarely leave Vannali or allow visitors.

Schools

After learning how to read, write, and do sums at their parents' knees, Weavers are assigned spirit tutors who help them undertake the necessary lessons to aid them in the life path they wish to follow.

Important places/buildings

Temples that enable communion with the spirits are scattered around the island and the most revered places on Vannali.

Standing Stones

Leading from the shore to the centre of Vannali, the Standing Stones guide and guard the way.

Trade goods

Spiritual healing   Cloth

Current Linked

Brinley

VANNALI

Celestial Bodies

Akaluo Belt

Visible from the Southern Hemisphere, the belt is home to the five brightest stars in the Lissaen sky.

Dalaples Cluster

A swarm of stars in the northern sky, this cluster can be seen swirling in blues and purples.

Kinsee

One of Lissae's moons.

Mublei Galaxy

Swirls of reds and purple decorate the western sky.

Omedis

An inhospitable planet ringed with debris and seven moons, Omedis is visible along the equator throughout most of the year.

Phior

Appearing as a bright green dot in the sky, this inhospitable planet appears in the Northern Hemisphere during the colder months.

Pomacanth Cluster

A constellation of stars found in the Lissaen sky depicting a fish.

Voil

A constellation visible when Lissae is near the Realm of Yaston.

Zaith

One of Lissae's moons.

Sulanta
Opestila
LISSAE
Vendalbara
Talhan
Vannali
Dee
Tevon
Rakemyst
Rohinda
Yaston
Vutana
Kenorvia
Fr
Jinkor
Nelonia
Muhara
The Shifting Islands of Lissae are constantly moving thro

Cantash
Lawrgaea
Nindonia
Ronah
Omina
Ginorti
Gondnotia
Akoren
Dento
Hulios
: waters. Their location is subject to change.

MEASUREMENTS

Distance & Speed

Clicks

A form of measuring speed. One click equals 1000 metres.

Time

Seasons & Months

Lissae has three months in each of the four seasons.

Days

Adonday	First day of the week.
Inthday	Second day of the week.
Kerday	Third day of the week.
Narday	Fourth day of the week.
Rasshday	Fifth day of the week.
Vebaday	Sixth day of the week.
Zoeday	Seventh day of the week.

Occasions

Natal day

The name used to describe the annual celebration of your birth. Typically a day enjoyed with friends and family, it is common to receive gifts enabling you to move into your next turn around the sun.

Spring Festival

Celebrated to acknowledge the return of spring, the festival is held on the first full moons after the flowers bloom. The use of drums is said to encourage new growth and is a time for all to come together to celebrate the survival of another winter.

Summer Eve

As the days draw longer, and the eve of summer approaches, bonfires on the beaches are lit at moonrise, offering warmth after a swim in the sea. More elaborate celebrations are held, where deities are honoured for the warmth they bring, and the crops they've bestowed. Feasts of fish crusted in salt are common.

Autumn Turn

As leaves change to orange, and the temperature dips, the crops are ready to be collected. Working throughout the day, beings from across Lissae help to harvest goods, and when night falls, they celebrate with a feast as they reflect on the blessings of the year.

Winter Frost

The full moons after the first frost of winter is a time for bonfires, gifting items to see others through the long cold, and making offerings of food to the spirits. This festival focuses on family and home, more than any of the others. To receive a gift at Winter Frost is to know that you hold a special place in the givers' life.

Joining

There are two main types that couples may choose between.

Soul matched couples may join before Lissae in a private ceremony that the Realm acknowledges. Such a joining is done in the home they will reside in, and automatically appears on a list of Joinings published by the local newspaper. It may never be rescinded or disbandoned.

A regular joining is usually preformed amongst family and friends, and is presided over by a Soul Innarnian. Such events are a cause of great joy. These bindings can be for a set time (a year and a day), for the rest of the couples lives, or for eternity. There is a theory that the last option is how Soul matched couples come to be.

NATURAL WORLD

Plants

Bereni tree

Common on the Shifting Islands, bereni trees are grown to house beings, with the middle of their trunks often being hollow.

Buta

A low growing shrub, the sprouts of the buta give the eater all the essential nutrients they require. What they hold in essence, they lack in taste, and are the most often refused food of the young or infirmed.

Crowfoot tree

Despite the black, spindly leaves, this tree produces delicious fruit.

Darfionious Oak tree

Only found in the Sephina Ranges, they house a special type of silkworm.

Hellewort

The perfect plant to help you sleep. Crush the small leaves to make a tea and sweeten with honey.

Julipa bud

Native to Lissae, this fleshy plant is notoriously difficult to maintain.

Pedutia

A large green, leafy plant that freezes well.

Rutenberry

A medium sized shrub, the rutenberry bush produces berries that delight a variety of beings.

Toslzura beans

A major crop on Lissae's Jinkor.

Toulana

A green vine with thin leaves and lots of tendrils that react to vibrations in the air and on the ground. Toulana is often planted to keep pests and birds away from the rest of the garden. The vine can distinguish between a positive or not-so-positive presence and can become overly friendly.

Wirri Leaf

A herb hung in the entranceways of Daen homes to keep the bad luck out.

Creatures

Arustos

A small mammal native to Cantash. These tree custodians live in hollows near the base of trees. They have a pointed snout, dirt-coloured scales, sturdy back legs, sharp teeth, and a strong tail. They use their forelegs to grab onto bugs, which their companion, Caelonis, fries for them.

Banded toe biter

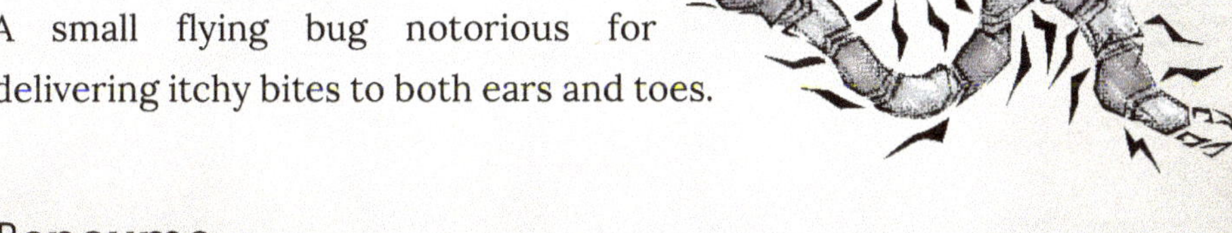

A small flying bug notorious for delivering itchy bites to both ears and toes.

Banoume

Wild desert beasts which inhabit Lissae. Of an equivalent size to Earth's elephants, the banoume have the temperament of a wounded hippopotamus.

Caelonis

A tiny bird native to Cantash. They can produce a jet of flame from their beaks. They typically use the flames to fry beetles for their arustos companions.

Draci

Tiny, dragon-like creatures that grow no bigger than a human's palm. The draci are native to Cantash, and those who have not found a being to bond with live in the gardens.

Dracovum

The hatchling stage of the **draci**.

Eobustus

Native to Cantash, the coal-black equines with manes of fire are a physical representation of energy and heat transference. They use heat from their surroundings to gather energy, then convert that energy into other things—movement, Innarn-boosting, galloping without rest. They are the fastest creature in all the Realms—provided they've had a good feed of magma or the sun is at full strength.

Esse

Tania's escape-artist chicken. Esse has blue feathers and a penchant for free-roaming well beyond her coop. She delights in exploring the surrounding neighbourhood, much to Tania's dismay and Collis's amusement.

Snack with blue feathers

Frito
Small, bird-like animal with wings similar to a dragonfly. They live their lives in the air, only returning to the ground to lay their eggs or die.

Gilagoats
Beasts bred for their strength. Gilagoats can carry large loads without strain.

Golem
A creature made of stone, dirt, or clay.

Hail
One of Cantash's draci.

Has claimed Shari as his human

It is odd to be claimed by a draci, but I don't know what I'd do if Hail hadn't tumbled out of that drain pipe.

Hantra

Earth spirits that are summoned. Given bodies made out of the earth, they are uncontrollable by the Shifting Islands. They are persistent and slow moving. Their only goal is to complete what the summoner has ordered them to do. The only way to kill a hantra is to remove both arms before decapitating it. Raising the hantra is taboo on any of the Shifting Islands.

Honeyhawk

Tiny birds native to Rakemyst. They have long, slender beaks and come in all colours of the rainbow. Typically travel in large flocks for protection.

Ignivas

Birds native to Cantash. The sparks their tails produce are used to heal the trees.

Jarnah Wasps

Luminous green and white-scaled wasps. Will chase and attack until their prey is out of their sight.

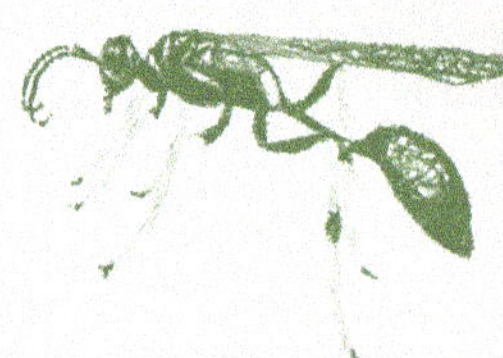

Ondirhund

A hound native to the mainland and prized for their exceptionally long hair.
See **Trade & Currency: Ondirhund Hair**

Palon

Native to Lissae, the palon is a small, six-legged creature descended from wolves. They have soft fur and long tongues, with a preferred diet of insects.

Parlock fish

Inhabit the shores off Ronah's northern beaches.

Phantom

Deep sea fish. Blue phantom is the easiest to obtain, but often has a tough, bitter flavour. Red phantom, although highly prized, is seen as cursed by sailors, who believe that those who touch the red phantom with bare skin whilst on the water will have their souls taken.

Pustish

Of **Vannali**. Creatures of myths, the pustish are tiny bats who are said to guard Spirit Innarn from misuse.

Risus

Black birds with a guttural laugh. Native to Tevon. Can be trained and used as messengers.

Shadow

Of Ronah. The only creature to be one of the Returned. See **Zoomer**. I'm not sure why he chose me, but I will be forever honoured I will also never tell Shari exactly how he came to be whole again

You know I read this too, right, Samuel? …

Shem'ar

Shem'ar are small dragon-like creatures, no bigger than a large dog and about as intelligent as canines. Kept most often as familiars, guard creatures, messengers, and family pets, shem'ar have soft, furry hides that come in almost any colour. Although incapable of using Innarn or talking, owners of the shem'ar can communicate telepathically with the creatures, some of whom understand more than others.

Sephina Silkworms

Small grubs that live in Darfionious Oak trees and produce the Realm's strongest cloth, sephina silk.

Sneeze

~~One of ~~ My draci. A menace to all.
Can you train them out of chewing on ears?

Sweetwater Bees

Small striped pollinator insects that make hives along riverbanks. They make honey with a salty tang.

Tuscaro

A small grey bird with a white beak, native to Vannali. This bird is said to only sing in true love's presence.

Vallan

A creature bred for its hide and meat. Vallan flesh is particularly delicious roasted.

Yuham

A milk-producing herd creature prized for its cheese.

Wisp

A **Shadow Bringer**, sent to watch over **Shari Dawn.** I don't care how much of a good idea you think it is, you should never, ever, send a shadow bringer to watch over someone.

Zoomer

~~Shari's palon~~ My palon The only creature to be one of the Returned. See **Shadow**. ☺

PEOPLE AND CUSTOMS

Lores

Creation

There are stories that span centuries of how Lissae came to be. Whispers of relics, of mortals becoming gods and leaving our Realm, and more.

These are all relegated to myth, along with the idea that, once upon a time, there was a protector like the Altoriae who bore a different title.

What we do know is that Lissae, unlike many other Realms, has a heart. And she chooses who guards that heart with great care, whispering into their ear a siren song sweeter than the notes that blow through falling leaves.

A song that can't be denied.

We may not know how Lissae came to be. But we do know how the Altoriae started. And here, in the Handbook, we deal with facts, not mere superstition.

Spirits

No spirit shall inhabit a second body until *after* they have moved on from the Spirit Realm. This Lore is to protect those who others wish to enslave. Most often used to enslave spirits are the Hantra and the Eni. Once in the flesh of these beings, the spirit who has been summoned has no control, as the being who calls the creature is the one who commands it.

All living and moving creatures have a soul and a spirit. This is to stop such creatures as the Hantra, the Eni, and others from consuming our Realm. These creatures need a spirit to function in Lissae, which means that only an available spirit can reside in one of these creatures and seeing as there are a finite number of spirits available, there is only a finite amount of these creatures that can exist in Lissae.

Immosa

The final resting place for the souls of warriors who left Lissae. Immosa is another name for the Spirit Realm that runs parallel to Lissae and is only able to be accessed by those who pass from the mortal coil upon Lissaen grounds.

Although little is known about this pocket Realm, it is theorised by many of our spirit scholars that Immosa must be separate from the main Spirit Realm, as those who agree to enter discussions do not know of the passing of those who have died around the same time as them. Others belittle the thought and assume that recent or concurrent deaths are just too hard to talk about.

That, and it's fun to keep the scholars guessing.

There can be so little amusement in the afterlife.

— Kay

Government

The governments of Lissae are similar for most mainland countries and follow the same basic format.

Mainland

President

Council of Elders (Between 6 - 45)

Mayor (of region)

Elders (Chosen from clans or are elected)

1 from each region on council

Occasionally, representatives of each country will meet, in which case, everyone from the Mayor up will be included.

Fixed Islands

The Fixed Islands are slightly different, with only a:

Prime Minister

Council of Elders

Mayor (of each island)

Elders

Mainland and Fixed Islands

When the Mainlands, Fixed Islands, and Shifting Islands meet, their representatives are:

Altoriae

Guardian

Presidents & Prime Minister

Ambassadors from Council of Elders

Shifting Islands + Wisara Representative

Council of Elders

Shifting Islands

Altoriae and/or Guardian
Council of Elders
Head Elder
Mayor
Elders
Heads Of Innarn

Portal Council

On the occasion that off-Realm fighting must happen, the following council will be called.
Altoriae and/or Guardian
Apprentice To The Guardian
Heads Of Army/Generals
Seconds/Sargent's
Patrol Leaders
Patrol Seconds
Patrol Groups
Trainees

Shari, you should really check this section.

Why? They never listen to me anyway.

Don't tell me you're trying to spoil her fun, Jonathan

She doesn't need any encouragement, Samuel. This is important.

And yet Shari has managed to defend Lissae without ever having to call the council... hmmm

Religion

Deities

Lissae has ~~six~~ seven deities who are said to have lived on the Shifting Island of Akoren.

Adeon

The God of the Element Fire and husband of Ke'ra.

Ke'ra

God of the Element Plasma and husband of Adeon.

Na'reh

Goddess of the Element Spirit and wife of Vebnah.

Rasshnae

Goddess of the Element Water and wife of Zoemer.

Vebnah

Goddess of the Element Air and wife of Na'reh.

Zoemer

God of the Element Earth and husband of Rasshnae.

Frainth

Forgotten Lissaen deity of Crystal. His statue can be found in Ronah's museum.

Once upon a time, when our world was new, there were three siblings. Adeon, he of fiery temperament and warm smiles; Zoemer, he who loved all things growing; and Vebnah, she who dreamed the days away with her fancies of flight.

Now, these three siblings met up with three others. There was Ke'ra, he who sparked at Adeon's slightest touch. Rasshnae, she who knew all the waterways on our new world, and Na'reh, she who could talk to the spirits who were bound to our land.

Ke'ra found Adeon's fiery temperament matched his, ember for spark. Rasshnae and Zoemer found love when they combined their interests, and Na'reh and Vebnah discovered that they shared a loathing of the spoken word but a love of silence that drew them together like nothing else could.

The three couples married on the eve of Lissae's first year as a Realm. Lissae almost became overwhelmed with the love between the couples and began to talk to them at night while they slumbered. Slowly, she told the couples what she wanted from them. She desperately needed someone to guide her people, and she knew these three couples were perfect for the task.

Ten years passed, and on the evening of their anniversary, the three couples met at Adeon and Ke'ra's hut. They discussed the things they had been dreaming of. After realising that they had been sharing the same dream, Adeon stood up and called to Lissae.

None were more surprised than he when the Realm answered him.

What happened next is shrouded in the mystery that is time, but what we do know is that six mortals had entered the hut, but it was six Deities who exited.

Adeon, with his warmth, became our God of the Element Fire. Ke'ra, his husband, became our God of the Element Plasma. Zoemer, with his love of growing things, became our God of the Element Earth, and his wife, Rasshnae settled by his side as our Goddess of the Element Water. Vebnah fulfilled her fancies and became our Goddess of the Element Air, with her wife, Na'reh, speaker to the dead, becoming our Goddess of the Element Spirit. They became the only six deities worshipped on our Realm, Lissae.

Innarn

(said Inn-*ar*-n) Predominately elemental magic which is present in all Realms to varying strengths. Innarn is split into three main groups: Dark, Grey, and Light. Each variant of Innarn has its own specialties. See **Elements** for more information. There are also other disciplines of Innarn, including Animal, Crystal, Mental, Realm, Techno, and Time.

Active

A term used to describe when a person's **Innarn** manifested and they became aware of it.

Blank

A person who can't use Innarn.

Bracelet

A bracelet is given to all tested Innarnians with beads the colour of the Innarn they are able to use. The brighter the bead, the more potential the Innarnian has for that element.

Glamour

A type of Innarn used to hide or disguise things. Typically cosmetic in application, glamours are favoured by those with heavy scarring or blemishes.

Innarnian

(said Inn-*ar*-ni-an) A person who can use Innarn.

Patrol

Any Innarnian resident over fifteen is required to help the Guardian and the Altoriae patrol the Realms to watch for any possible threats.

Piggyback

Mentally piggybacking is something that telepathic Innarnians can do. It is a way of gathering information and listening to conversations. It can be stopped by strong mental shields.

Rassu

People who claim to be Innarnian, but who use trap doors, sleight of hand, and tricks to reproduce the effects of what a real Innarnian can do.

Send/Sent

The word used for telepathic communication.

Shifting

The Innarn art of teleportation from one space to another.

Wards

Innarn shields designed to protect specific areas.

Disciplines

Elements

Lissae has seven main elements that Innarnians can manipulate:

Air	Crystal	Earth
Fire	Plasma	Spirit
Water		

However, there are also five other disciplines:

Animal	Mental	Realm
Techno	Time	

Below are tables of the sub-disciplines of each group. (Please note that some disciplines show up in multiple places)

Air

Air Ball	Air Trap	Incendiary Cloud
Airboat	Airy Water	Shape Change
Air Cage	Alteration	Ride the Wind
Airy Constrictor	Conjure Elemental	Wall of Ice
Air Control	Death Fog	Weather Manipulation
Air Creations	Far Sight	Whispering Wind
Air Double	Fly	Wind Blast
Air Healing	Gust of Wind	Wind Wall
Air Shields	Ice Storm	

Animal

Animal Alteration	Animal Conjuring	Animal Manipulation
Animal Control	Animal Healing	Charm Animal

Crystal

Holds energy which is turned into electricity. Often installed in clusters to gain more power and last longer. Different coloured crystals do different things. White Crystals are used for communication. Black Crystals gather power and Orange Crystals connect currents to create fences. Crystal necklaces are given to young children and Blanks for them to manipulate the Crystals.

Crystal Cage	Crystal Creations	Crystal Shields
Crystal Control	Crystal Healing	Prismatic Wall
Technomancy		

Earth

Alteration	Flower Bloom	Shift Earth
Charm Plants	Fist of Stone	Shift Lava
Conjure Elemental	Lava Flow	Shift Sands
Earth Ball	Lava Storm	Shift Stone
Earth Breathing	Lava Suit	Sand to Earth
Earth Cage	Lava to Fire	Stone Shape
Earth Control	Move Earth	Stoneskin
Earth Creations	Plant Care	Stone to Lava
Earth to Stone	Plant Growth	Stony Grasp
Earthen Grasp	Plant Heal	Turn Pebble to Boulder
Earth Healing	Plant Repair	Wall of Iron
Earth Shields	Reverse Gravity	Wall of Sand
Earth Trap	Rock to Mud	Wall of Stone
Earthen Constrictor	Seedling Care	Water to Sand
Earthen Double	Shape Change	Weather Manipulation

Fire

Alteration	Fire Healing	Lava to Fire
Burning Hands	Fire Shields	Lightning to Fire
Conjure Elemental	Fire Trap	Minute Meteors
Delayed Blast Fireball	Fire to Water	Plasma to Fire
Fire Ball	Fiery Constrictor	Pyrotechnics
Fire Breathing	Flame Arrow	Shape Change
Fire Burst	Flame Fist	Shift Lava
Fire Cage	Flaming Sphere	Turn Ember to Fire
Fire Control	Incendiary Cloud	Wall of Fire
Fire Creations	Lava Flow	Weather Manipulation
Fire Double	Lava Storm	
Fire Flow	Lava Suit	

Mental Disciplines

Alarm	Fear	Power Word, Stop
Animalism (communicate and connect with animals)	Feeblemind	Power Word, Stun
Armour	Feign Death	Precognition
Astral Projection	Forcecage	Programmed Illusion
Ancient Curses	Forget	Project Image
Anti-Innarn Shell	Fumble	Protection
Aura Perception	Globe of Invulnerability	Psychoanalysis (studying the unconscious mind)
Avoidance	Guards and Wards	Remove Curse
Banishment	Hallucinatory Terrain	Repulsion
Bind	Healing	Safeguarding
Blending (to blend in with surroundings)	Hold Person	Scare
Blindness	Illusionary Script	Screen
Blink	Innarn Missiles	Secure Shelter

Blur	Innarn Weapon Enhancer	Seeming
Chain Contingency	Innarn Weapon user Enhancer	Shades
Chaos	Invisibility	Shape Change
Chaos Shield	Imprisonment	Shatter
Charm Animal	Innarn Armour Enhancer	Shielding
Charm Monster	Heightened Senses	Shocking Grasp
Charm Person	Levitate	Silence Self
Cone of Cold	Lifetime Binding	Slow
Confusion	Lower Resistance	Speed
Creeping Shadow	Magic Mirror	Spell Immunity
Darkness	Mass Charm	Spell Turning
Deafness	Mass Shield	Stabilize
Delude	Mass Suggestion	Steal Enchantment
Disintegrate	Mesmerize/ Hypnotize	Strength
Dispel Innarn	Mind Blank (a.k.a. Brain Fart II)	Suggestion
Divination	Mind Fog (a.k.a. Brain Fart I)	Taunt
Dream	Minute Meteors	Telekinesis
Emote (manipulate others' emotions)	Mirror Image	Telepathy
Empathy	Misdirection	Teleportation
Enchant an Item	Mass Invisibility	Unbreakable Shield
Enchanted Armour	Mislead	Unshakable Curse
Enchanted Weapon	Non-detection	Veil
Energy Drain	Permanent Illusion	Wall of Force
Ensnarement	Power Word, Blind	Wildshield
ESP (Extra Sensory Perception)	Power Word, Speed	Wildstrike

Plasma

Acid Arrow	Plasma Constrictor	Plasma to Fire
Acid Storm	Plasma Control	Plasma Trap
Alteration	Plasma Creations	Plasmatechnics
Conjure Elemental	Plasma Double	Storm Control
Lightning Hands	Plasma Fist	Water to Plasma
Lightning to Fire	Plasma Flow	Weather Manipulation
Lightning Control	Plasma Healing	Shape Change
Plasma Ball	Plasma Shields	Wall of Plasma
Plasma Cage	Plasma Storm	

Realm Disciplines

Airboat	Hold Being	Shadow Walk
Alteration	Levitate	Shielding
Astral Projection	Portal Creation	Summon Being
Conjuration	Realm Travelling	Shifting Living Creatures
Dimension Door	Receiving Living Creatures	Shifting Objects
Demi-shadow Monsters	Receiving Objects	Shifting Self
Extension	Sending Living Creatures	Vortex Creation
Far Reaching	Sending Objects through Realms	Weather Manipulation
Fly	Sending Souls through Realms	
Gate Creation	Shadow Door	

Spirit Disciplines

Alteration	Heightened Senses	Spirit Armour
Astral Projection	Hold Undead	Spirit Cage
Aura Perception	Mesmerize / Hypnotize	Spirit Control
Blending (to blend in with the surroundings)	Pfortitude (resistance to psychic damage)	Spirit Healing
Dominate (ability to command another)	Possession	Spirit Shields
Empathy	Shape Change	Spirit Summoning
Healing	Spectral Force	Spirit Wall

Techno Innarn

Crystal Control	Technomancy

Time Innarn

Slow Time	Stop Time	Travel Forward
Speed up Time	Travel Back	

Water

Airy Water	Turn Droplet to Lake	Water to Dust
Alteration	Wall of Ice	Water to Plasma
Conjure Elemental	Water Ball	Water to Sand
Fire to Water	Water Breathing	Water Trap
Ice Storm	Water Cage	Watery Constrictor
Lower Water	Water Control	Watery Double
Part Water	Water Creations	Waveform
Rock to Mud	Water Flow	Weather Manipulation
Shape Change	Water Healing	
Shift Water	Water Shields	

Motus

The movement used to create Innarn. One must have thought, intent, and movement correct for the Innarn to work. Motus can be an individual construct, or a widely recognised form.

Forms of motus used: Sleep; **Wind Blast**; Wall of Stone

General Motus

These can be adapted to suit any Innarn, so long as the elemental movement is correct.

Innarn Ball

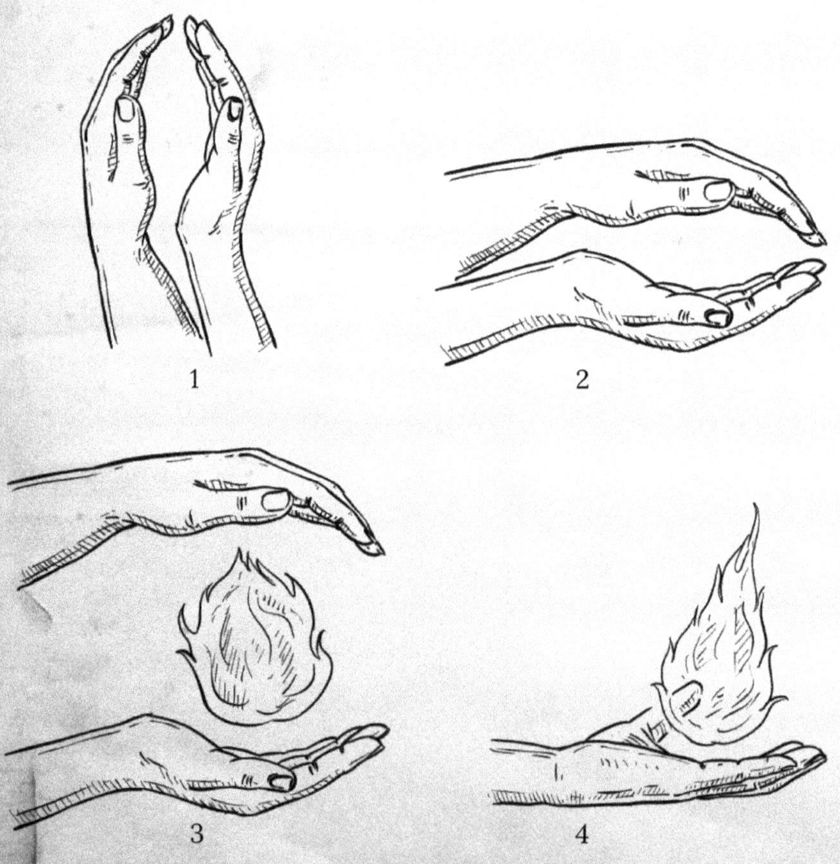

Innarn Cage

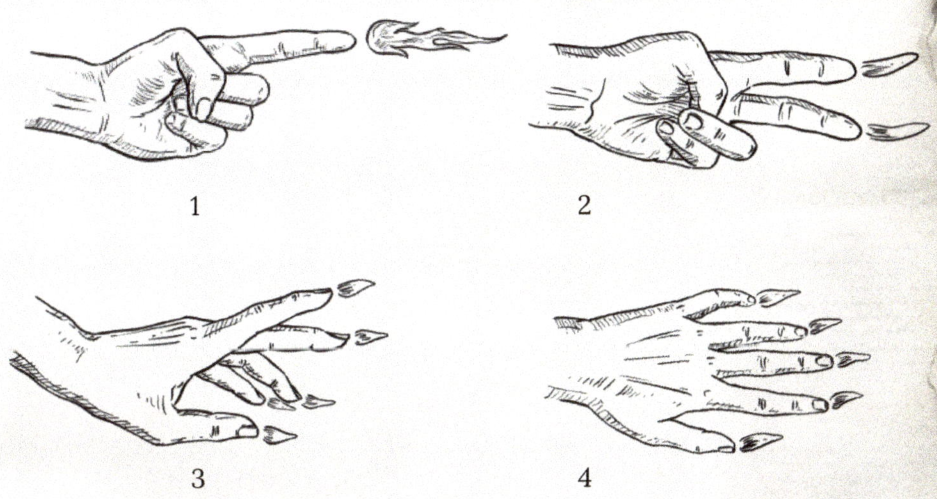

Innarn Shield

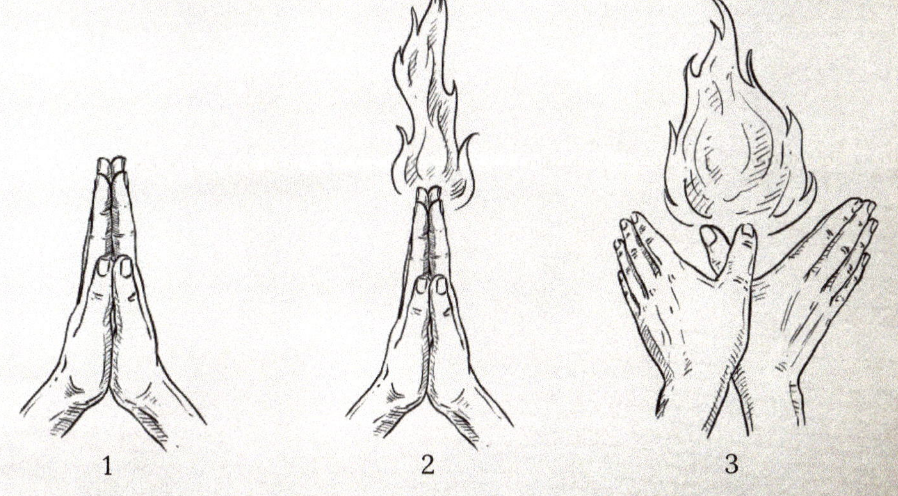

Innarn Wall

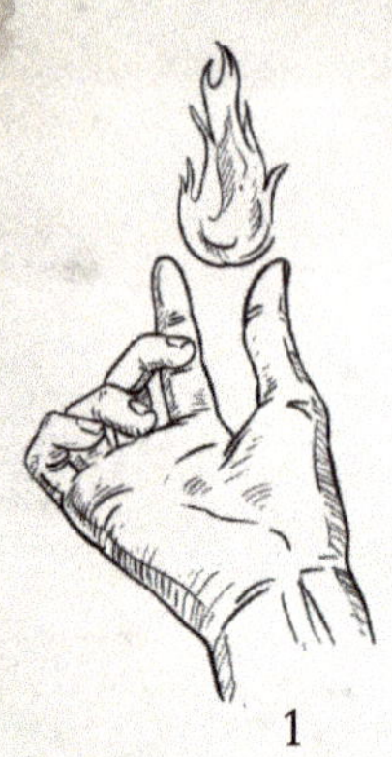

1

2

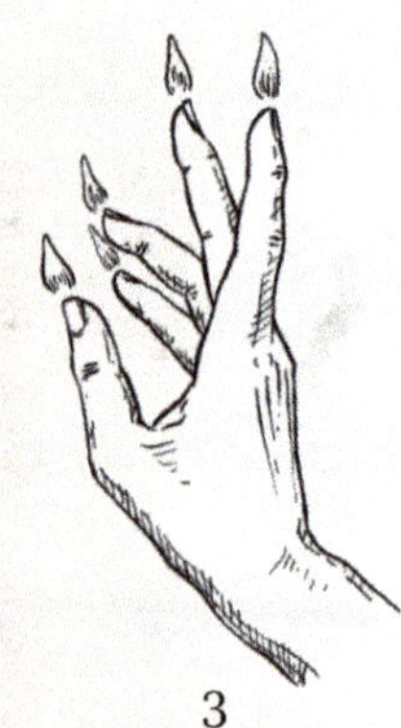

3

4

Innarn Warding

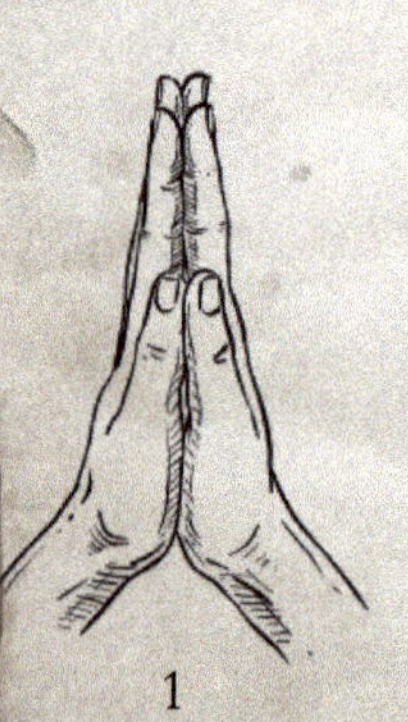

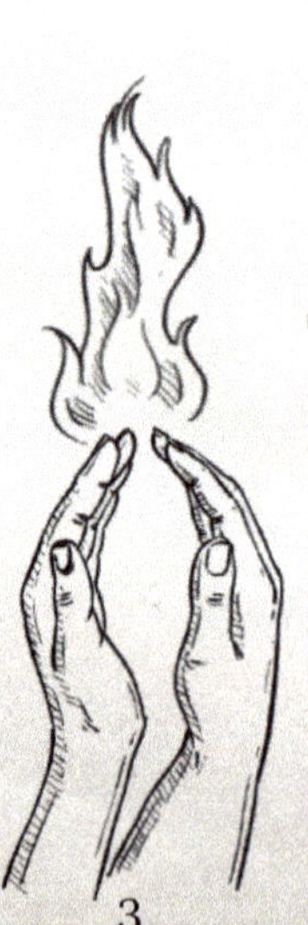

1

2

3

Air Motus
Wind Blast

An eighth-year Elemental Innarn **motus** used to blast and/or flatten objects with Air Innarn.

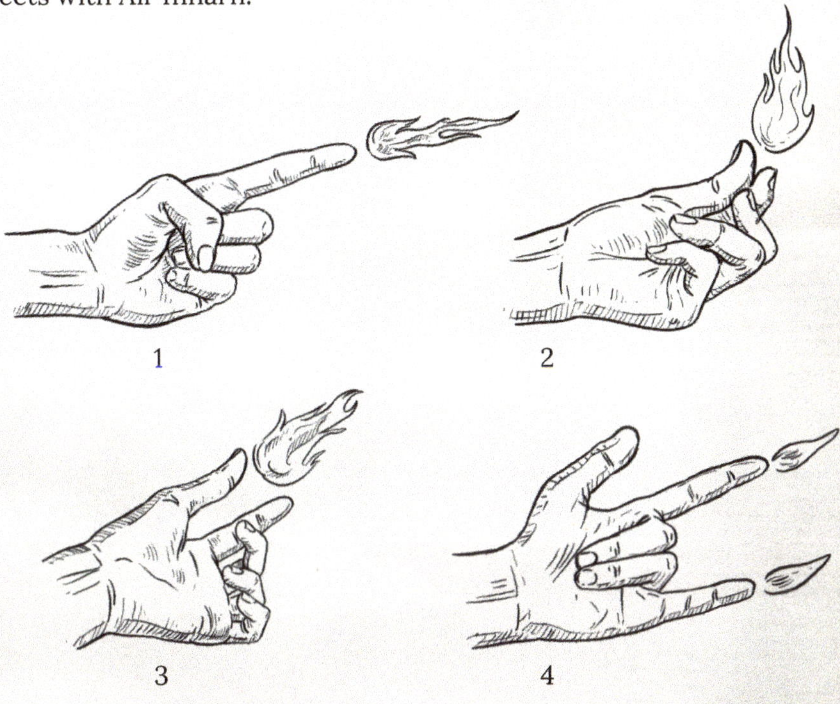

Animal Motus
Charm animal

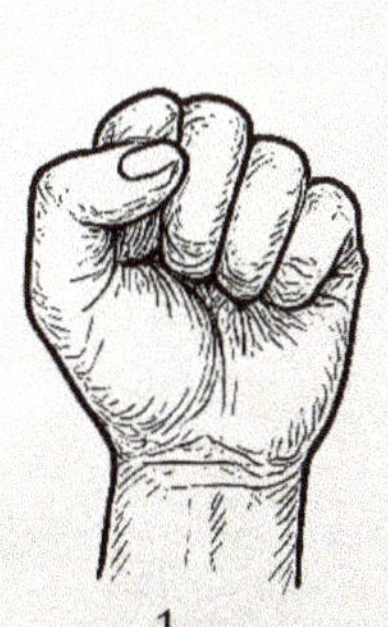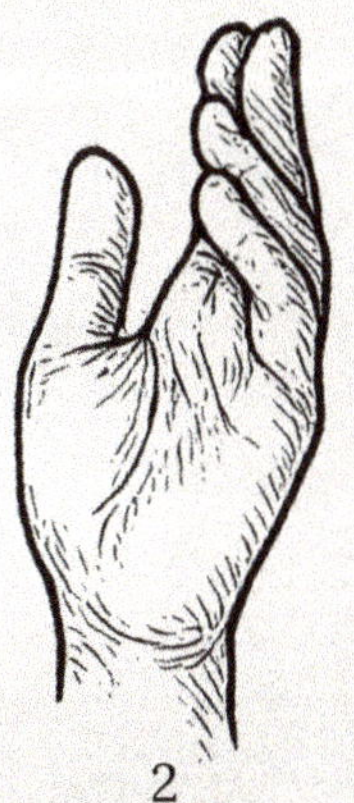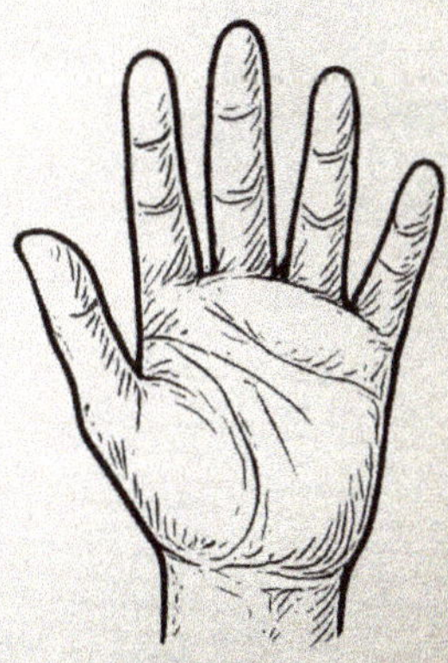

Schooling

As children usually begin to show Innarn around two years of age, Innarn lessons begin around four years of age. 'Normal' schooling begins around five years of age. Schooling of all types usually finishes at seventeen years of age, unless an individual wishes to further their education in a particular field.

Teachers are typically referred to by the honorary "Tutor" and their last name. Speciality teachers, such as oral history tellers, are referred to as "Lore Keepers".

Normal Schooling subjects include:

Art	Healing	Music
Cooking	History	Nature Studies
Craft	Language (native and one other)	Science
Dance	Maths	Sports
Drama	Metalwork	Woodwork

Students on Ronah can also study:

Animals	Deities	Realms
Crystal Energies and Power Sources	Mapping	

Innarn Schooling subjects include:

Animalistic Innarn	History of Innarn
Astral Projection	Meditation
Aura Reading	Nature Innarn
Conjuration	Rules regarding use of Innarn
Control of Innarn	Sight – Far, Future
Crystal Innarn	Telekinesis
Divination	Telepathy
Elemental Innarn	Time Innarn
Empathy	Transmutation Innarn

Enchantment with Innarn

Healing with Innarn

Travelling Innarn

Weather Manipulation

Students on the Shifting Islands can also study:

Advanced Healing

Defensive Innarn

Group Defensive Innarn

Group Offensive Innarn

Grouping with Innarn

Offensive Innarn

A Breakdown of School Subjects on the Shifting Islands

Animalistic Innarn	1st Year Physiology of Animals Psychology of Animals Animals with Innarn Animals without Innarn 2nd Year Communication with Innarn Animals Communication with Non-Innarn Animals	3rd Year Conjuring Inter-Realm Animals Conjuring Outer-Realm Animals 4th Year Healing Animals Animal Growth

Astral Projection	**1st Year** Astral Spell Far Reaching I Extension I Far Reaching II Extension II **2nd Year** Far Reaching III Extension III Far Reaching IV Extension IV Contact Other Realm	**3rd Year** Far Reaching V Extension V Fabricate Far Reaching VI Extension VI **4th Year** Far Reaching VII Extension VII Sending Objects, Small Sending Objects, Large **5th Year** Shifting Soul/s through Realms
Aura Reading	**1st Year** Aura Sight What Colours Mean What Areas Mean Aura Reading of Animals Aura Reading of Humans **2nd Year** Aura Reading of Weavers Aura Reading of Ilutri Aura Reading of Da'mar Aura Reading of Centaurs Aura Reading of De'tora Aura Reading of Daen Aura Reading of Lat'ra	**3rd Year** Aura Reading of Lut'ru Aura Reading of Simino Aura Reading of Tes'mra Aura Reading of Santae Aura Reading of Oushlat Aura Reading of Ousmal Aura Reading of Fret'aro **4th Year** Aura Reading of Elementals Aura Reading of Light Beings Aura Reading of Neutral Beings Aura Reading of Dark Beings

Conjuration		
	1st Year Minor Creation Faint Light Mirror Image Spook Unseen Servant	**5th Year** Faithful Companion Major Creation Shadow Monsters Monster Summoning IV Shadow Innarn
	2nd Year Continual Light Dismissal Monster Summoning I Phantom Steed Spectral Hand	**6th Year** Innarn Mount Instant Summons Invisible Tracker Monster Summoning V Summon Shadow
	3rd Year Chaos Shield Illusionary Wall Minor Globe of Invulnerability Monster Summoning II Stinking Cloud	**7th Year** Day to Night Intensify Summoning Monster Summoning VI Night to Day Shadowcat
	4th Year Conjure Elemental Monster Summoning III Spectral Steed Tangled Web Watery Double	**8th Year** Maze Monster Summoning VII Phantasmal Killer Summon Swarm Symbol
		9th Year Trap the Soul

Control of Innarn	Every Year – This is a part of the curriculum for every Innarn Student	
Crystal Innarn	1st Year Different uses of Crystal 2nd Year Caring for Crystal 3rd Year Cleaning Crystal	4th Year Finding Crystal 5th Year Installing Crystal
Divination	1st Year Detect Innarn Detect Undead Identify Detect Evil Detect Invisibility 2nd Year Detect Scrying ESP Detect Alignment Locate Object Past Life	3rd Year Clairaudience Clairvoyance Contact Other Realm Divination Enhancement False Vision 4th Year Foresight Freezing Sphere Locate Creature True Seeing Vision

Elemental Innarn

1st Year	**5th Year**
Elements	Earth Shield
Elementals	Fire Shield
Elemental Innarn	Water Shield
Air Charm	Air Trap
Earth Charm	Earth Trap
Fire Charm	Fire Trap
Water Charm	Water Trap
	Tempest
2nd Year	Ice Storm
Affect Normal Fires	Lava Storm
Burning Hands	Turn Pebble to Boulder
Fire Burst	Turn Droplet to Lake
Fist of Stone	Turn Ember to Fire
Pyrotechnics	
Earthen Grasp	**6th Year**
Flaming Sphere	Air Double
Ride the Wind	Fire Breathing
Whispering Wind	Fire Double
	Wall of Fire
3rd Year	Wall of Ice
Shift Sands	
Shift Earth	**7th Year**
Shift Stone	Airy Water
Shift Lava	Conjure Elemental
Shift Water	Earth Breathing
Sand to Earth	Earthen Double
Earth to Stone	Stone Shape
Stone to Lava	Waveform
Lava to Fire	
Fire to Water	**8th Year**
Water to Sand	Fiery Constrictor

	4th Year	Watery Constrictor
	Air Ball	Airy Constrictor
	Earth Ball	Earthen Constrictor
	Fireball	Wind Blast
	Water Ball	Lower Water
	Fire Flow	Move Earth
	Gust of Wind	Part Water
	Lava Flow	Water to Dust
	Rock to Mud	
	Water Flow	9th Year
	Stony Grasp	Delayed Blast Fireball
	Water Breathing	Flame Fist
	Watery Double	Lava Suit
	Wind Wall	Stoneskin
		Air Travel
Empathy	1st Year	3rd Year
	Antipathy-Sympathy	Shielding Others (mentally)
	2nd Year	4th Year
	Shielding Yourself (mentally)	Shielding Groups (mentally)

Enchantment with Innarn

1st Year	**7th Year**
Charm Person	Domination
Friends	Dream
Hypnotism	Feeblemind
Taunt	Hold Monster
Whispering Wind	Seeming
2nd Year	**8th Year**
Bind	Enchanted Weapon
Blindness	Ensnarement
Blur	Mass Suggestion
Forget	Mislead
Invisibility	Programmed Illusion
3rd Year	**9th Year**
Creeping Shadow	Permanent Illusion
Hold Person	Project Image
Illusionary Script	Repulsion
Levitate	Shades
Strength	Veil
4th Year	**10th Year**
Charm Monster	Lifetime Binding
Confusion	Forcecage
Emotion	Mass Charm
Spectral Force	Sink
Suggestion	Steal Enchantment
5th Year	**11th Year**
Enchant an Item	Chain Contingency
Fumble	Energy Drain
Hallucinatory Terrain	Stabilize

	Magic Mirror	Unshakable Curse
	Secure Shelter	Ancient Curses
	6th Year	
	Advanced Illusion	
	Airy Water	
	Chaos	
	Cone of Cold	
	Demi-shadow Monsters	
Healing with Innarn	1st Year	3rd Year
	Patient Care I	Colds
	Anatomy	Flu's
		Common Minor Ailments
	2nd Year	Uncommon Minor Ailments
	Scratches	Diagnosing I
	Dislocations	
	Healing Bones	
	Sleep I	
	Temporal Stasis	
History of Innarn	1st Year	3rd Year
	Our Realms History	Neutral Realms History
	2nd Year	4th Year
	Light Realms History	Dark Realms History
Meditation	1st Year	3rd Year
	Sense Shifting	Pain Removal
	2nd Year	4th Year
	Astral Projection	Higher Self

Nature Innarn	1st Year Plant Care Seedling Care Plant Growth Plant Repair Plant Heal	2nd Year Flower Bloom Charm Plants Reverse Gravity 3rd Year Weather Innarn is the next part of the Nature Innarn Course
Rules regarding use of Innarn	**Every Year –** This is a part of the curriculum for every Innarn Student	
Sight – Far, Future	1st Year Far Sight (current Realm) 2nd Year Extended Far Sight (off Realm)	3rd Year Future Sight (days to weeks) 4th Year Future Sight (weeks to years)

<table>
<tr>
<td rowspan="2">Telekinesis</td>
<td>

1st Year
Moving Small Objects I
Moving Medium Objects I
Moving Large Objects I

2nd Year
Moving Small Grouped Objects I
Moving Medium Grouped Objects I
Moving Large Grouped Objects I

3rd Year
Moving Small Objects II
Moving Small Grouped Objects II
Moving Medium Objects II
Moving Medium Grouped Objects II
Moving Large Objects II
Moving Large Grouped Objects II

4th Year
Moving Small Objects III
Moving Small Grouped Objects III
Moving Medium Objects III
Moving Medium Grouped Objects III
Moving Large Objects III
Moving Large Grouped Objects III

</td>
<td>

5th Year
Moving Small Objects IV
Moving Small Grouped Objects IV
Moving Medium Objects IV
Moving Medium Grouped Objects IV
Moving Large Objects IV
Moving Large Grouped Objects IV

6th Year
Moving Small Objects V
Moving Small Grouped Objects V
Moving Medium Objects V
Moving Medium Grouped Objects V
Moving Large Objects V
Moving Large Grouped Objects V

7th Year
Mass Telekinesis

</td>
</tr>
</table>

Telepathy	1st Year Clairaudience	5th Year Tongues
	2nd Year Comprehend Languages	6th Year Conversation I Short, two people
	3rd Year Contact Other Realm	Conversation II Long, two people Conversation III Short, multi-person
	4th Year Message	Conversation IV Long, multi-person Conversation V Indefinite

Time Innarn

1st Year	5th Year
Slow Time I	Slow Time V
Speed Up Time I	Speed Up Time V
Stop Time I	Stop Time V
Travel Back I	Travel Back V
Travel Forward I	Travel Forward V
2nd Year	6th Year
Slow Time II	Slow Time VI
Speed Up Time II	Speed Up Time VI
Stop Time II	Stop Time VI
Travel Back II	Travel Back VI
Travel Forward II	Travel Forward VI
3rd Year	7th Year
Slow Time III	Slow Time VII
Speed Up Time III	Speed Up Time VII
Stop Time III	Stop Time VII
Travel Back III	Travel Back VII
Travel Forward III	Travel Forward VII
4th Year	
Slow Time IV	
Speed Up Time IV	
Stop Time IV	
Travel Back IV	
Travel Forward IV	

Transmutation Innarn		
	1st Year	**7th Year**
	Glorious Transmutation	Distance Distortion
	Chill Touch	Fabricate
	Colour Spray	Passwall
	Dancing Lights	Shadowy Transformation
	Enlarge	Stone to Flesh
	Feather Fall	
		8th Year
	2nd Year	Duo-Dimension
	Fist of Stone	Permanency
	Lasting Breath	Prismatic Spray
	Mending	Prismatic Sphere
	Metamorphose Liquids	Statue
	Spider Climb	
		9th Year
	3rd Year	Alter Self
	Deeppockets	Vanish
	Fog Cloud	Shape Change Objects
	Shatter	Shape Change Living Beings
	Strength	Shape Change Self I
	Wall of Fog	
		10th Year
	4th Year	Shape Change Self II Same Size
	Explosive Runes	Shape Change Self III Bigger
	Haste	Shape Change Self IV Smaller
	Infravision	Shape Change Self V Different
	Invisibility, 10' Radius	Race
	Transmutate Item	Shape Change Self VII
		Different Species
	5th Year	
	Secret Page	**11th Year**
	Slow	Shape Change Self VIII Object

	Water Breathing Wraith form 6th Year Improved Invisibility Massmorph Secure Shelter Rainbow Pattern Solidify Fog	Shape Change Self IX Permanent
Travelling Innarn	1st Year Dimension Door Hold Portal Levitate Receiving Small Objects Shift Small Objects 2nd Year Ride the Wind Receiving Medium Objects Shadow Door Shadow Walk Shift Medium Objects	3rd Year Fly Receiving Large Objects Shift Large Objects Receiving Living Creatures Shift Living Creatures 4th Year Airboat Gates Shift Self Shift Without Error Vortex

<table>
<tr><td rowspan="2" style="writing-mode: vertical-lr">Weather Manipulation</td><td>

1st Year
Understanding of Weather
Patterns
Autumn
Winter
Spring
Summer

2nd Year
Lightning Bolt
Minute Meteors
Rain
Ride the Wind
Wind Wall

3rd Year
Cyclones
Chain Lightning
Freezing Sphere
Hail
Part Water

</td><td>

4th Year
Acid Storm
Earthquake
Meteor Swarm
Tsunami
Wind Blast

5th Year
Wild Weather
Wild Fire
Wild Wind
Wild Rain
Wild Lava

</td></tr>
</table>

<table>
<tr><td rowspan="18" style="writing-mode: vertical-rl">Advanced Healing</td></tr>
<tr><td>1st Year</td><td>4th Year</td></tr>
<tr><td>Sleep II</td><td>Repair Lungs</td></tr>
<tr><td>Sleep III</td><td>Repair Heart</td></tr>
<tr><td>Sleep IV</td><td>Repair Brains</td></tr>
<tr><td>Sleep V</td><td></td></tr>
<tr><td>Animate Stasis</td><td>5th Year</td></tr>
<tr><td></td><td>Arthritis</td></tr>
<tr><td>2nd Year</td><td>Cancer</td></tr>
<tr><td>Patient Care II</td><td>Common Major Ailments</td></tr>
<tr><td>Common Ailments</td><td>Uncommon Major Ailments</td></tr>
<tr><td>Uncommon Ailments</td><td></td></tr>
<tr><td>Diagnosing II</td><td>6th Year</td></tr>
<tr><td></td><td>Minor Genetic Conditions</td></tr>
<tr><td>3rd Year</td><td>Major Genetic Conditions</td></tr>
<tr><td>Repairing Organs</td><td></td></tr>
<tr><td>Repair Vision</td><td>7th Year</td></tr>
<tr><td>Repair Hearing</td><td>Minor Conditions</td></tr>
<tr><td></td><td>Major Conditions</td></tr>
</table>

Defensive Innarn

1st Year	7th Year
Alarm	Confusion
Armour	Fear
Guards and Wards	Earth/Fire/Water Shield
Protection From Evil	Wind Wall
Shield	
	8th Year
2nd Year	Improved Invisibility
Bind	Minor Globe of Invulnerability
Blindness	Secure Shelter
Blur	Minor Spell Turning
Chaos Shield	Remove Curse
Darkness, 15' Radius	
	9th Year
3rd Year	Avoidance
Deafness	Mind Fog (a.k.a. Brain Fart I)
Mirror Image	Safeguarding
Misdirection	Silence Self
Protection from Normal Missiles	Stoneskin
Protection from Paralysis	
	10th Year
4th Year	Anti-Innarn Shell
Blink	Globe of Invulnerability
Delude	Wall of Force
Dispel Innarn	Wall of Iron
Scare	Wall of Stone
Shatter	
	11th Year
5th Year	Forcecage
Enchanted Armour	Mass Suggestion
Feign Death	Mind Blank (a.k.a. Brain Fart II)
Hold Undead	Mislead

	Innarn Armour Enhancer Invisibility, 10' Radius 6th Year Non-detection Protection from Evil, 10' Radius Protection from Innarn Missiles Slow Spirit Armour	Wildshield 12th Year Banishment Imprisonment Prismatic Wall Unbreakable Shield Mass Shield Screen Spell Immunity
Group Defensive Innarn	1st Year Chaos Shield Mirror Image Misdirection Protection From Projectiles Scare 2rd Year Delude Dispel Innarn Non-detection Safeguarding Wall of Iron	3rd Year Anti-Innarn Shell Globe of Invulnerability I Guards and Wards Secure Shelter I Wall of Force 4th Year Globe of Invulnerability II Wall of Stone Mass Invisibility Mass Shield Secure Shelter II
Group Offensive Innarn	1st Year Scare Dispel Innarn Minute Meteors	

Grouping with Innarn	1st Year Mass Telekinesis	
Offensive Innarn	1st Year Dispel Innarn Innarn Missile, Small Acid Arrow Flame Arrow Minute Meteors 2rd Year Enchanted Weapon, Small Air Trap Earth Trap Fire Trap Scare 3rd Year Shocking Grasp Water Trap Innarn Missile, Medium Enchanted Weapon, Medium Enchanted Armour	4th Year Disintegrate Innarn Weapon Enhancer Innarn Weapon user Enhancer Innarn Armour Enhancer Lower Resistance 5th Year Acid Storm Death Fog Forcecage Flame Fist Incendiary Cloud 6th Year Energy Drain Power Word, Stun Power Word, Blind Power Word, Stop Power Word, Speed Wildstrike

Guilds

General Guild Rules

- You must be 18 years of age or over to become a member of a guild.
- The guild elders have the right to accept or decline any application.
- Upon receiving your approved application, you shall receive either:
  - One year of advanced training, followed by three years of supervision by a guild member.
  - Or two years of basic training, followed by one year of advanced training and three years of supervision by a guild member.
  - If, during this time, you decide that the guild you have chosen is not right for you, you may request to be removed from the guild after an acceptable notice period (between a month and one year).
  - The guild does not have the right to deny removal from the guild.
  - The guild, however, does have the right to request your removal at any time, after an acceptable notice period (between one month and one year).
- Guilds may require members to retain certain information pertaining to the guild—this may include signing a pact stating that they will not divulge or discuss sensitive information to entities not amongst their guild members.
- Guilds have an obligation to their members to provide for them in times of hardship.
- Guild members are required to tithe between 1% and 10% of their income to their guild. The guild elders set the tithing amount for each member. If a member disagrees with the amount they have been requested to tithe, there are processes they can embark on—both within and outside of the guild.
- Each guild may have a set of rules it requires its members to follow. Each guild will also have a set way to deal with members who disregard their rules.

- Guilds are required to supply any instruments, tools, and clothing members require for their work as well as any replacements which members may require.
  - There may be a set number of replacements, or a time frame limit for replacements as well as a small cost involved for materials that are required outside of these limits or numbers. These things will be mentioned either in the guild rules or in the agreement you sign when your application is approved.
- Guilds may have sub-guilds, which members may switch between. Members may be required to undertake further training before switching into or from a sub-guild. Members may also be required to apply to the guild elders to switch into or from sub-guilds. These applications may be granted or denied by the elders.

Current Guilds

Assassins Guild

An unofficial guild that is never mentioned and rarely spoken about, they work to keep the political climate of Lissae on a somewhat even keel.

If one were to peer into the darkest of corners and the correct time, one could potentially find someone to take care of that pesky problem in a way that would be untraceable.

Carers Guild

Started by the friend of a burnt-out carer, this guild is mostly made of those who support others who care for those who can no longer care for themselves. Found in all parts of Lissae, this guild is one of the larger ones.

Chefs Guild

Anyone who professionally prepares food for others can apply to be part of this guild. They regularly take in trainees to learn a variety of skills, including meals, cakes, baked goods, desserts, and more.

Crafters Guild

Perfect for those who use their hands to create, the Crafters Guild has a variety of sub-types, which are mostly separated by material, such as wood, metal, fibre and stone.

Note that the Crafters Guild is distinct from the Repairers Guild, as the former creates the original product, while the latter merely fixes it.

Crystal Guild

This guild covers the Innarn use of crystal. Almost all the members attend Talhan for training.

Talhan's current Linked has fought for all Crystal Innarnians to be part of the guild, but has been overruled by the Technomancer.

Entertainers Guild

One of the larger guilds, its members are found on every part of Lissae. This guild arguably has the fewest restrictions on members, with their ethos being: if you can entertain someone, you belong with us.

Farmers Guild

If you grow crops or raise animals, you can be part of the Farmers Guild. Meetings are in the middle of all seasons, except during harvest/birthing times. Members are encouraged to share information that will help others in producing healthy plants and animals.

Fauna Guild

Aimed at those who care for non-farm animals, the Fauna Guild ensures the health of the creatures under the care of its members. They are also frequently called to help wildlife that has been involved in accidents.

Flora Guild

Aimed at those who grow no-crop plants, the Fauna Guild ensures that the biospheres of Lissae are correctly maintained.

Healers Guild

Perfect for those who feel the pull to heal others, rather than rend them from tip to toe. They are distinct from the Fauna Guild as they heal beings, rather than creatures, although occasionally you will get an Innarnian who is adept at both.

Lawmakers Guild

Credited with enforcing the decision of the Elders, the Lawmakers are found on the mainlands and Fixed Islands of Lissae.

Lissae Guild

Charged with looking after the entire Realm of Lissae. Members are mostly made up of Innarnians who patrol the various gateways.

Ronah's Guild

Sub-guild of the Lissae Guild—focuses on protecting and looking after Ronah.

Protectors Guild

Sub-guild of the Lissae Guild—focuses on protection.

Altoriae's Guild

Sub-guild of the Lissae Guild—focuses on aiding and protecting the Altoriae.

Core member list

Shari Dawn	Jonathan Buan	Samuel Caragnton
Alistair Hollingsworth	Collis	Lira
Amara	Daivi	Mu
Amauran	Dealon	Raven
Ashlen	Elani	Remmy
Asterion	Fiona	Talofa
Belfar	Joana	Tania Hollingsworth
Benny	Kieran	Wolf Dawn

Mariners Guild

Made up of sailors, fishermen and those who work and live on the sea, the Mariners Guild sail all the waters of Lissae.

Muses Guild

Distinct from the Crafters and Entertainers Guilds, the Muses Guild offers elite membership to writers, musicians and artists who typically perform their creative works solo.

Repairers Guild

Separate from the Crafters Guild, the Repairers Guild focuses on reclaiming items and fixing them, with a strong focus on sustainability.

Shopkeepers Guild

If you have a shop on Lissae, you are automatically a candidate for the Shopkeepers Guild! Well met and welcome. We meet monthly to discuss stock rotation, shoplifting deterrents, and all sorts of other interesting information. *The most boring meetings I shall ever attend. I'd prefer to down an entire bottle of Ornaian wine than sit in one again.*

Teachers Guild

Created for educators of the young, old and everyone in between, the Teachers Guild meets during term breaks to go over curriculum content. There is a consensus across Lissae that they are not paid enough for their work in teaching the next generation.

Tech Guild

Put together by the Technomancers of Talhan, the Tech Guild shares in depth tips and tricks to better harness your Techno Innarn. Creations are regularly shared and improved upon, and membership is limited to those Temira can stand to be around.

Thieves Guild

The less said, the better, unless you want your pockets empty before you realise they were full in the first place.

Travel Guild

This guild covers travel by air, water, and land.

A specific subset of the guild, known as 'Travel Innarnians' are set up in offices in most ports and main towns. For a substantial fee, you could sit in a cushy capsule and be transported anywhere on Lissae. They use Air Innarn to follow the currents and transport people, livestock, and things across vast distances. The object or being travelling is placed on the landing platform, either alone or in a capsule. The Air Innarnian checks the streams and currents, then sends them to the destination. It is not, despite what most think, instantaneous. This form of travel can be quite dangerous, particularly over long distances.

Lissae's seas are difficult to cross at the best of times, and travel between the continents is best done below the waves or well above the highest spray.

Travelling under the seas is predominantly done with the Wisara, who know Lissae's oceans better than anyone.

Food & Drink

Artuian Broth

A green broth Healers use on patients with internal burns.

Azehal

A drink favoured by the current Guardian. A rutenberry-flavoured stimulant drink, typically served with sweetener and milk.

Buta sprouts

A small, round root vegetable that tastes like ten-day-old socks.

Calromata

Red, opaque berries with the approximate heat level of lava. Native to Cantash and favoured by the Daens.

Citrus butter

Made with the rind and juice of citrus mixed with butter to make a creamy, spreadable blend.

Daborang

A spiced tea with a citrus tang of Yessna's making. Flavoured with honey.

Gilfress Elixir

Made from the roots of the gilfress plant, the elixir was created by Zana, Rakemyst's Linked. It has the colour of honey and viscosity of water. It has a spicy scent and acts as a pick-me-up for the drinker.

Iccecot sorbet

A tart, sweet sorbet native to Akoren. Served in small glass bowls, and typically decorated with cream, berries and citrus slices, the sorbet has an alcoholic component. Strongly recommended consuming in moderation.

Kunun soup

Thick orange soup served with plates of crisped bread.

Lukkorel

A large, edible fungus native to the Shifting Islands of Lissae. This mushroom is large enough to use as a bowl and eat it afterwards. Best pan-fried or slow-cooked.

Orbisalium

A large apple-like fruit. The pale blue skin of the ripe fruit indicates a delicious crispiness, whereas the green skin of the juvenile fruit denotes toxins strong enough to cause gastrointestinal upsets or, if consumed in large enough quantities, death.

Osin berries

Small, sweet yellow berries. Can be used to make a delicious zingy drink.

Persea

A green stone fruit, native to Ginorti. Goes well spread on toast with a touch of lemon and salt.

Quass juice

A sweet bubbly orange drink, served cold.

Rutenberry

The frosted, dark-purple skin of the rutenberry hides the chocolate-like fruit inside. It can be eaten raw, although the skin can be bitter. Skinned, mashed, and cooked, it can be added to cakes, biscuits, and other sweets, including drinks.

Sand pears

A juicy fruit native to Lissae's Shifting Islands, it is favoured by many.

Solfruit

Palm-sized fruit with crisp, blue skin and a creamy-coloured, crunchy flesh. Native to the Shifting Islands of Lissae.

Soola

A green, leafy vegetable that can be eaten raw or cooked with butter and herbs. Its musty taste can be improved by adding salt and a sprinkle of Innarn.

Telmi

A savoury herb native to Rakemyst. It has a similar flavour to spicy spring onions and a stunning deep orange leaf. It is quite tasty in a variety of dishes, including savoury muffins.

Toslzura beans

A major crop on Lissae's Jinkor.

Xobrac

A sweet, purple juice.

Yaqueona

An oblong-shaped red, gourd, best served stuffed or roasted. Native to Cantash.

Yuham cheese

Cheese created from the milk of the Yuham.

Sports & Games

Archery

Played as both a solo game and a group, archery doubles as a sport and a training exercise. Solo players aim to score as many points in a target as possible. Groups can be either pairs, where one aims at a target behind their teammate with points removed for every flesh hit, or with four beings, where players must traverse a field and take turns in hitting the centre of the targets in their part of the field.

Fencing

Unlike the equivalent sport in other Realms, fencing had become so bloodthirsty that it was forbidden on Lissae after Marius Defanza beheaded and de-limbed his opponent in under ten seconds before a crowd of thirty thousand spectators. Their match had not yet started. When the referee called foul, Marius gave the woman the same treatment. It is purported that it took three dozen beings to subdue the bloodthirsty fencer, and lest it happen again, the elders across Lissae passed their first unanimous vote to outlaw the sport.

Nimble Surfing

An Innarn sport played on a large field. Players ride boards and attempt various death-defying stunts. Each stunt earns points. The highest score wins. Falling from the board is an automatic disqualification. Nets are used for learners but are discarded in professional competitions.

Sennet

A board game that originated with the Egyptian people of the Realm of Earth, and a favourite game of Elder Thorne of Ronah.

Trade & Currency

Books and Newspapers

Like all great Realms, Lissaens enjoy a variety of stories. Some of the titles featured within the series include:

Amoka

Read to discover the gardener's journey to find just the right plants to grow on an island that can traverse all the different climates on Lissae.

Beginners Guide to Innarn

Starting your journey into discovering your Innarn? This is for you.

Cultivating your Island Garden

Written for residents of the Shifting Islands by our very own Harmony Thorne, this is the book you need to ensure your crop can survive in every climate.

Guide to the Realms

Written by Resa Sunab, Guardian of the twelfth Altoriae, this is a must read for any of the Protectors Guild.

Hekkor Mafae

A book about Dark ones that Jonathan is very uncomfortable about having on Lissae. It updates as the Dark Conclave delegates agree on the discussion topics, and helps the Chair to keep on track, despite the madness. Samuel has banished it to his personal pocket Realm. *(Again)*

Sailors Guide to Changing Seas

The perfect guide to sailing Lissaen oceans.

The Sea Tailor's Handbook

The most boring book in existence. Not even worth a second glance.

The Shifting Island Sentinel

The major source of news for The Shifting Islands of Lissae. Available on your crystal slab with the low-cost subscription of 3 ziom beads a day! Also referred to as the *Sentinel*.

Tales of Tillamirus

Ancient tales that follow Tillamirus on an exciting adventure.

Cosmo shell

The pearlescent shell of a deepwater crustation native to Lissae. Used in decorative objects and jewellery. Incredibly expensive because of the difficulty of harvesting the shell from the long-lived creatures.

Hemibise

Iridescent stones which glow in the presence of starlight.

Ondirhund Hair

Up to two metres long, the hair of the hound is used for a variety of things, including bowstrings, ropes, and more.

Sephina Silk

Collected from silkworms that feast on the Darfionious Oak tree, which is only found in the Sephina Ranges. It produces the warmest, softest, strongest fabric, and there's something about it that makes it immune to Fire and Water Innarn.

Ziom

The hardest metal in the Realms, found on Lissae. Used in the creation of housing frames, precious jewellery, currency, and weapons.

Ziom Beads

A form of currency on Lissae.

Technology

B.I.R.D.

Stands for 'Bio Instructor for Relative Distance'. Designed by Xani of Talhan to ensure beings would stop bumping into things if they were absorbed in their crystal slab. The B.I.R.D. device acts as both a guide and a guard.

B.I.T.

A Basic Innarn Training device created by Temira of Talhan. This device is designed to test the user's abilities without anyone else getting hurt.

I'm sorry — this is a killing machine. It literally killed me. How is that a 'test'?!

Temira did apologise. Kind of.

Oh yes, terribly sorry for killing you, would you like another?

That's not an apology, that's attempted assassination.

Attempted being the key word.

Crystals

Holds energy which is turned into electricity. Often installed in clusters to gain more power and last longer.

Crystal See and Speak Communications

Or CS&SC. Also called Crystal Send. Similar to Earth's videophones.

Crystal Video Screen

Or CVS. Similar to Earth's televisions.

Farscope

A device predominantly used by sailors and explorers on Lissae to view things at great distances.

Femto-crystals

The latest in healing technology for Talhan. They can help a patient recover from any damage they've sustained and decrease recuperation time. After a disastrous accident involving Atlantian technology mixing with the femto-crystals, research was pushed back significantly, however, the benefits still bear consideration.

Null Crystal

A crystal crafted by mainlanders which suppresses the use of Innarn so much that Innarnians are unable to access their innate talents.

Words & Phrases

Aberration

A slur used by mainlanders to refer to **Innarnians**.

Aqua ineas

A phrase used to counter the bad luck of stepping into a puddle.

Boon

Something that is granted for a completed task or heroic deed.

Buta Sprout Wars

A Hoffman household tradition.

Capsule Trip

Wealthy Lissaens may choose to travel via capsule when needing to traverse long distances. While they still need to visit a Travel Innarnian, the trip is usually far more comfortable.

Cedore

A curse used by Samuel. Also used as: slime-filled cedore. See **Curses**.

Crystal Slab

Smaller slabs are used for newspapers and other serial publications. Larger versions can be used as viewing screens or furniture.

Curses

Several curses are common on Lissae, including: Adeon's Fire; By the Life of Lissae; Ke'ra's Flash; Zoemer's Rocks; Rasshnae's Floods; Vebnah's Breath; Na'reh's Ghosts.

Dark One

A term used to describe beings from the Darkest of Realms.

Fizzpot

An insult used by the older generations.

Healers

Similar to Earth's doctors, they heal patients who are sick or injured, usually using Innarn. Although they also use the old methods.

Hekkor Mafae

A book about Dark ones that Jonathan is very uncomfortable about having on Lissae.

Hello

An outdated greeting, considered rude by the current population.

Hin

A teddy bear belonging to **Mu** in his younger days.

Hospital

Also called **Healers Centre**. A place to go when sick or injured.

I bid thee well

A traditional phrase when two or more people part ways.

Kinaesthesis

The sensation by which bodily position, weight, muscle tension, and movement are perceived.

Lissaen

A person who lives on Lissae.

Mainlanders

A name for those residing on the mainland or fixed islands of Lissae.

Mother Realm

The only Realm capable of giving birth to new Realms. Highly guarded and sought after.

Pocket Realm

A small Realm that is attached to a larger one.

Portal

The place between Realms, guarded by the **Ducibus**. Also referred to as the **Ducibus' Hall**.

Proprioception

Perception or awareness of the position and movement of the body.

Risen

The name given to those who formally resided in Lissae's **Spirit Realm** and are now residents of Carilla.

Sentient

Able to perceive or feel things, capable of thought and communication.

Spirit Realm

A Realm that is found alongside Lissae, where the spirit or souls of the deceased go when their physical bodies are no longer needed.

Tales of Lore

Held by the Lore Keeper and told during lessons or ceremonies, the Tales of Lore explain the beginnings of Lissae and life on our Realm, as well as important events and the exploits of the Altoriaes, as has been passed down through the ages. See: **Lore Keeper**

Technomancer

The head of the **Techno Centre** of **Talhan** has been given the nickname of technomancer due to the number of times her advances have brought the seemingly deceased back to life.

Veti Cant

Or Cant, is a sign language that uses hands and facial expressions to communicate. It is often helpful when overcoming language barriers. There are variations for beings with more limbs, but the essentials of the Cant remain the same.

Well Met

A traditional greeting throughout the Realms.

Widdershins

To turn in an anti-clockwise direction.

Ze/Zir/Zim

Gender-neutral pronouns.

Zhahyeem

An expression meaning, 'Be calm'.

Beings of Lissae

A

Abby Thorne

The eleventh Altoriae. She lived until she was 91 years old when she died from an attack. One of the Risen.

Aharny

An Ilutri Travel Innarnian, formerly working out of Dento.

Ailan

Guardian of the seventh Altoriae.

Aisling

Guardian of the tenth Altoriae.

Alan Pratt

Mayor of Ronah.

Alistair Hollingsworth

Of Ronah. Son of Liza, stepson of Jordan. Brother to Jessica, Christopher, Caleb, Sorsha, and Tania. Former candidate for the Guardian's Apprentice.

Growing up on the mainland, Alistair didn't realise he was an Innarnian until after he and his family moved to Ronah. As a child, he had a rather traumatising experience, which locked his Innarn away more successfully than any of the mainlanders realised.

When his stepsister, Tania, became Ronah's Linked, his Innarn started to unfurl, until psychic backlash due to too many beings sending at once totally unlocked the block.

Amara Telka

A Daen, currently of Ronah. Formerly of Cantash. Former candidate for the Guardian's Apprentice. Adopted by **Gus** after an attack resulting in the death of her parents.

A student of the Daen academy, she worked to master her Fire Innarn. She occasionally struggled with her control due to an excess of power.

Her preferred weapon is an axe which is half her body weight and height. Air Charms help to lift it in fight mode.

New member of the Altoriae's Guild.

Credited with the death of the former leader of the Chirea, Amara did her best work when she was part of the Altoriae's Guild.

Her favourite food is calromata sauce.

How does she manage to constantly trip over air? This girl is danger on two legs. Deceased due to catching a chakram with her skull. The best idea is not to catch a chakram at all. Just let it sail by

Amauran

Of Ronah. One of the Returned, and a member of the Altoriae's Guild.

Amelia

Of Freehorne. Jonathan Buan's aunt. After learning of her brother's cursed death, she threw Jonathan out of her house to prevent the misfortune from spreading.

Ana

See **Askanar**.

Andrew Shansky

Of Ronah. Father of Eric Shansky, husband of Louise Shansky.

Anika Thorne

Of Ronah. Daughter of Rany Thorne. Anika grew up being the most popular girl on Ronah and was usually Shari's preferred subject for practicing her Innarn by projecting it to happen in front of Anika in order to maintain the illusion that Shari was a Blank. The Elders of Ronah became convinced Anika was the long-awaited thirteenth Altoriae.

Aiming to live up to her parents' exacting standards, Anika made a deal with an U'tan for a small amount of Innarn. She was able to levitate light objects.

After a run-in with Anriluka, her Innarn was stripped away and she became a Blank.

Determined never to be a victim again, Anika started leaning on her strengths. She became Shari's stylist and learned how to defend herself.

I thought my family was bad, but then I met those who were meant to protect this hatchling. They've done a lousy job of it. She seems determined to dress more than just Shari. Anika designed clothing for the Guardian and myself, and even Shari's stabby cousin. She does it all with a grace that belies her rough start to life.

Anna

Of the Spirit Realm. Formerly of Ronah. Former protector of the museum.

Antya

Of Talhan. One of the patrol leaders.

Arilla Dawn

Of Ronah. Mother of Shari Dawn, wife of Calem Dawn. Owner of the Quiver and Quill Tavern.

Arilla had to learn how to defend and fight at a young age and chose the blade. She's a master at swords and blades of most types. **Anika Thorne** came to her for lessons, and those grew to encompass many beings who either lacked Innarn or felt that they needed more to protect themselves, particularly in times where Innarn would fail them without warning.

Shari learned the blade at her mother's side and was able to keep up with Arilla by the time she was eleven.

Nice enough. For a Blank. Very sorry about the arrow. I was aiming for your daughter.

Ashlen Shansky

Of Ronah. One of the Returned, and a member of the Altoriae's Guild. Uses a spiked cudgel.

Askanar

The third Altoriae. She lived until 121 years old, when she died in an attack.

Asterion

Formerly of Atlantis. Formerly known as Archer Terion. A professor who donated his mind to become myth embodied. Currently of Ronah. One of the **Returned**.

Azulie Von Dayme

Of Ronah. Guardian of Petuar, the second Altoriae. Talented artist.

B

Becky Ribeck

Of Ronah.

Belfar

Of Rakemyst. Mate of Wolf Dawn. Second in command of Elder SilverCloud's guards.

Ben

Of Kenorvia. Elder.

Benny

Of Ronah. One of the Returned.

Berrimon

Of Talhan. One of the patrol leaders.

Brayden

Of the Wisara. A spokesperson.

Bren

A Weaver from Vannali. A candidate for the Guardian's Apprentice.

Bryon

Of Ronah. One of the patrollers. Friend of Kaya Silverstone. Helped find an incapacitated Guardian Buan when he was patrolling Tuklopia.

Briar

Of the mainland. Tried to assassinate Guardian Buan.

Failed. Twice in a row. What are they teaching assassins these days?

Brinley

Of Vannali. Weaver. Vannali's Linked.

C

Caeli

Of Akoren. Former candidate for the Guardian's Apprentice. Soul-matched to **Domic Iabor**.

Caleb Hollingsworth

Of Ronah. Son of Jordan, stepson of Liza. Brother to Jessica, Christopher, Alistair, Sorsha, and Tania.

Calem Dawn

Of Ronah. Father of Shari Dawn, husband of Arilla Dawn, son of SilverCloud, and brother of Wolf Dawn. Owner of the Quiver and Quill Tavern.

Firstborn son of an elder and a Linked, Calem chose his name to reflect his love of his very human mate.

His younger years were spent learning how to become an Ilutri priest. Instead, he left with Arilla to raise their daughter on Ronah.

A protective father, Calem showed his love through food, making sure Arilla and Shari ate balanced diets that were absolutely delicious.

He sacrificed everything to keep Shari safe. I can respect that.

Calem and Arilla Dawn

The best parents ever.

Captain Rappen

Of Jinkor. Under Elder Chamele's command.

Chamele

Of Jinkor. Elder. Extreme bias against Innarnians (who she called aberrations). *Dead. Couldn't have happened to a more horrible being.*

Charin

Of Rakemyst. One of the patrol members in Wolf's group. Spouse of Varlee.

Christopher Hollingsworth

Of Ronah. Son of Liza, stepson of Jordan. Brother to Jessica, Alistair, Caleb, and Tania.

Cian

Husband of Lerah, fifth Altoriae. Deceased.

Ciaran

Of Talhan. A Blank with a scarred face.

Clara

Guardian of the eighth Altoriae.

Collis Iuvo

Of Ronah. Unofficial leader of the Returned. Sworn guardian and soul-match of Ronah's Linked. Member of the Altoriae's Guild.

Crista Davis

The ninth Altoriae. She lived until she was 32 years old when she died via an attack. One of the Risen.

Crystal Intelligence

Of Lissae and Atlantis. *Should say—of trouble and mayhem. Never trust a talking crystal. And for the love of the Nine Hells, never take a machine from Atlantis!*

Cyrus Petram

Of Talhan. Talhan's Linked.

D

Daivi

Of Ronah. One of the **Returned**.

Danielle Williams

Shari Dawn's great grandmother. Arilla Dawn's grandmother.

Dealon

Currently of Ronah. Formerly of the Wisara. Former candidate for the Guardian's Apprentice. New member of the Altoriae's Guild. *Can even make vegetables taste delicious.*

Denesska

Of Ronah. Innarnian architect. One of the **Returned**. Favours a double-headed war hammer.

Domic Iabor

Of Akoren. Akoren's Linked.

Drah

Of the U'sala. Twin brother to Kerk. Formerly of **Duhiomel**.

E

Edward Thorne

Of Ronah. Husband of Harmony. Elder of Ronah. Grandfather of Anika Thorne. Missing limb regrown by the thirteenth Altoriae before she was announced.

Elani

Currently of Ronah. Formerly of Ginorti. Former candidate for the Guardian's Apprentice. Member of the Altoriae's Guild.

Elder Ovi Ribeck

Of Ronah. Elder of Ronah. One of the **Returned**.

Elder Prilla Thorne

Of Ronah. Elder of Ronah. One of the **Returned**. Can create crystals.

Elder Ribeck

Of Ronah. Elder of Ronah. Patrol Leader,

Elder Shansky

Of Ronah. Elder of Ronah.

Elder SilverCloud

Of Rakemyst. See **SilverCloud**.

Elder Silverstone

Of Ronah. Elder of Ronah.

Elder Stewart

Of Ronah. Elder of Ronah.

Eli Thorne

Of Ronah. Student at Ridden Hall.

Elizabeth (Liz) Ribeck

Of Ronah. Student at Ridden Hall. Named after her aunt, Lizbeth. Classmate of the thirteenth Altoriae.

Ember Sparks, Professor

Of Cantash. Head of Ignis Academy, Professor Sparks looks barely older than his students.

Eminlith

Guardian to Kay'imi. She married the first Thorne who arrived on Ronah, Timony. Eminlith's ruby pendant has been passed down in the Thorne clan for generations.

Eni Anderson

How Shari refers to the Eni that took over Lawrence Anderson.

Eric Shansky

Of Ronah. Son of Louise and Andrew Shansky. He frequently goes missing. The youngest **Returned**. Favours Asterion.

Esme

Of Talhan. Former candidate for the Guardian's Apprentice, Esme is considered the best Air Innarnian around. Her favoured weapon is the bow.

Estaban

Of Lissae. Patrol member who worked with Mu.

Estebar

Guardian of the fifth Altoriae.

Eva

Of Cantash. Formerly of Talhan. Orphaned. Former femto-crystal tester. Looks after those who have no one else to turn to. Now works at **Books 'n' More**.

Everon Castor

Author of the bestseller *From Ember to Flame*. *Good to know I can do something other than hurt beings.*

F

Felton

Of Ronah. Formerly of the U'sala. Explosives expert.

Fenix

Of Cantash. Daen. Cantash's Linked.

Feyla

The fourth Altoriae. She lived until she was 153 years old.

Fiona

Of Ronah. A travelling scout for the Guardian of Lissae.

Fiona MacAde

Formerly of Ronah. The twelfth Altoriae. She took up the title in 3981 at ten years of age. She lived until she was 24 years old, when she died from an attack.

Fortesque

Travel Innarnian. Formerly of Lawrgaea. Currently residing on Talhan.

G

Garayen

Of the Wisara. An elder. Dealon's grandfather.

General Morrow

Of Ginorti. Head of the Satyrs' army. Father of Liza Morrow. Grandfather of Tania Hollingsworth.

Gerrard

Patrol leader and member of the Mariners Guild.

Ginna

Of Lissae. Reporter for *The Shifting Island Sentinel*.

Golden Priest

See **Sanithane**.

Grace

Of Jinkor. On the death of her mother, she was taken by the mainlanders. Former slave of Chamele. Rescued and brought to Ronah. Cousin to the thirteenth Altoriae's cousin. Formerly known as **Lissa**.

Likes stabbing family I can relate to that.

Gus

Of Tevon. Adopted Amara Telka after the death of her parents.

Gwyn

Of Vendalbara. Elder.

H

Halfair

Of Ronah. One of the **Returned**.

Haran

Of Dento. A Kumaru. Former candidate for the Guardian's Apprentice.

Harmony Thorne

Of Ronah. Talented Earth Innarnian. Wife of Edward. Grandmother of Anika Thorne. Loves carrot stew. Teaches Shari about plants.

Healer Edwards

Of Ronah. Healer.

Healer Holli Doonavan

Of Ronah. Head Healer. *Would often do what is right for her patients, despite orders from others who pretend to be higher in rank. She's a healer. There is no higher rank.*

Healer Ribeck
Of Ronah. Healer.

Henot
Of Ronah. Formally of the **U'sala**. Gnome. Has a friendly rivalry with **Kibon**.

Hensey
Of Ronah. Kay'imi's nephew. Son of Shania.

Humans
Humans are often called the base model for the other races. There seem to be two main types of humans—those with Innarn and those without, although the two remain physically the same. Quite often they live in large groups—cities or towns—mostly to interact with others.

They do not seem to mind the other beings or creatures of Lissae, but there are a small number of them who are close-minded. Thankfully, these types of humans seem to stay together.

Overall, the Humans are friendly and personable, although not much different from any of the other races.

I

Ian
Of Lissae. Member of the Mariners Guild. Innarnian in charge of fishing sailors out of the water. Rescued Jonathan Buan when he was flung off the boat by a violent storm as a boy.

Ifera
Formerly of Ioyitmar. Granddaughter of Whitmore.

Indijo
Of Ronah. Collis's childhood best friend.

Ishta

Of Jinkor. Part of the mainlanders' troops. New Innarnian.

Ira

Of Lissae. A spirit who helps Talofa train to become the next Guardian's Apprentice.

Isabelle

Of Ronah. One of Jonathan's original patrollers, and partner of Drew.

J

Jali Thorne

The tenth Altoriae. She held the title for three years, before being trampled by a herd of ullfin.

Jamie

Of Tevon. Lira's younger brother.

Jeran Metasta Voutar

Of the U'sala. Former leader. Deceased.

Jessica Hollingsworth

Of Ronah. Daughter of Jordan, stepdaughter of Liza. Sister to Caleb, Christopher, Alistair, Sorsha, and Tania.

Jetonyx

Of ~~Altorit~~ Ronah. Kin to Samuel. *Golden Q'Avalide. Potential farmer.*

Jillon

Of Talhan. Elder.

Joana

Of Ronah. One of the Returned. Mother of Tobias. Currently running the **Quiver and Quill Tavern.**

Jonathan Michael Buan

Of Ronah. Formerly of Freehorne. Formerly known as Jon. Son of Michael Buan. Jonathan fled to Ronah after his father's death and became apprentice to the Guardian at only 8 years old. After watching the previous Guardian be eaten by a Q'Aralide he took up the title. In 4053, he became the Guardian of Shari Dawn, the thirteenth Altoriae.

When he's not saving the Realm, Jonathan owns and runs **Books 'n' More**, a store on Ronah.

He has issues staying alive on his own Realm. And befriending dubious beings. Oi! Hush, you know you're one of us now. The Realms may just freeze over. The Altoriae and the Guardian both trust me. Who knew it would take a new Realm to loosen the Guardian up?

I can always punch you again? Pass.

Jordan Hollingsworth

Of Ronah. Husband of Liza, father of Caleb, Christopher, Alistair, Tania, and Jessica. Deputy headmaster of Ridden Hall.

Joshua Izzaya Clemisc

Of the Spirit Realm. Formerly of Ronah. Former Guardian. Was considered one of the most brutal Guardians due to his lack of compassion for his apprentices, of which, he lost many. Killed by the Q'Aralide.

Julian

Of Ginorti. Trained in the same class as Elani.

Juniper

Of Talhan. Head Elder of Talhan and the link between the young and old.

K

Kamdon

Of Ronah. One of the **Returned**.

Kaya Silverstone

Of Ronah. Patrolled with Guardian Buan when he was still an apprentice.

Kay'imi

The first Altoriae. She lived until she was 1217 years old, when she was killed by a lone Ahana archer.

Kemanyr

Newest Q'Aralide. *Recently hatched. With colours. And a penchant for escaping. Golden, loves ritenberries and embarrassing her elders.*

Kerk

Of the **U'sala**. Twin brother to Drah. Formerly of **Duhiomel**.

Kibon

Of the **U'sala**. Long-range weapons expert. Has a friendly rivalry with **Henot**.

Kieran

Of Ronah. Brother of Sean. One of the Returned.

Kodan

Formerly of the U'sala. *Can rot in the bowels of an acid pit for all eternity. Has somehow managed to redeem himself. Colour me shocked.*

Kris Hoffman

Of Ronah. Mitchel Hoffman's younger brother.

Kym McMullin

Of Ronah.

L

Larn

Of Talhan. One of the patrol leaders.

Larrian

Of Lissae. Was Peadar's patrol partner when he died and was revived by the technomancer.

Laura

Of Ronah. A student from Ridden Hall with exceptionally Dark Innarn for one born on Lissae. *Tiny little Dark thing. Actually concerned for my safety. Under my protection. Don't even think about hurting her.*

Lawrence Anderson

Of Ronah. Former Headmaster of Ridden Hall. *Killed by the Eni in 4049.*

Headmaster Anderson is the one death which occurred on Ronah that I could not personally prevent. There are nights where I dream of meeting him on the first day of school, and he changes into the Eni who took him over, and I can't do anything to stop it.

I didn't even know of the Eni before they tried to take over Lissae. Can't say that I'm happy I had to end them all, but when they were determined to infest every last Lissaen, I didn't have a choice.

Lerah

The fifth Altoriae. She lived until she was 334 years old when she died due to an attack.

Lerryn

Travel Innarnian.

Liadain

Of Ginorti. A Satyr. Guardian of sixth Altoriae. One of the Risen.

Lira

Currently of Ronah. Formerly of Tevon. Former candidate for the Guardian's Apprentice. Member of the Altoriae's Guild.

Lissa

Sarina's daughter. Niece of Arilla Dawn. Cousin of Shari Dawn. Now known as **Grace**.

Liza Hollingsworth

Of Ronah. Daughter of General Morrow. Wife of Jordan, mother of Caleb, Christopher, Alistair, Tania, and Jessica. Headmaster of Ridden Hall.

Liz Ribeck

See: **Elizabeth (Liz) Ribeck**.

Lizbeth Ribeck

Of Ronah. My friend Hurt her and you won't live to see another sunrise. I will rip you into tiny pieces, bathe you in acid, and blend what's left into a drink. Go on, try it. I'm thirsty I will peel your skin off, piece by piece, and make you watch while I rip your still-beating heart from your body The hatchlings called her sweet treats, and she heard. Never have I been more mortified

LoneWolf Dawn

See **Wolf Dawn**.

Louise Shansky

Of Ronah. Mother of Eric, wife of Andrew Shansky.

M

Maddie

Of Freehorne. Assistant to the former Travel Innarnian.

Maeve Riley

Of Ronah. Student at Ridden Hall. Gossip queen.

Mara Ribeck

Of Talhan. Formerly of Ronah. Healer of optics. Augmented sight. Niece of Lizbeth Ribeck. Chose her career to help her favourite aunt.

Marcus

Of Freehorne. Bigot.

Max

Of Ginorti. Part of the Satyrs' army.

Maxian

Of Lissae. Brother to Arilla Dawn and Sarina.

Mayor of Ronah

See **Alan Pratt**.

Met'sara

First Guardian of Kay'imi, the first Altoriae.

Meyron

Of Rakemyst. Felled in the initial attack by the Chirea. Used to have a golden feather.

Michael Buan

Of Freehorne. Jonathan Buan's father. Deceased.

Mick

Of Cantash.

Milo

Of Cantash. Self-appointed secretary to Cantash's Linked. Deceased, twice.

Miss Jo

Of Freehorne. Librarian *and the kindest person on the Realm.*

Mitchel Hoffman

Currently of the Spirit Realm. Formerly of Ronah.
Former Guardian's Apprentice. Also called Mitch. Friend
to Shari Dawn. Sadly missed by all who knew him.

At 15, Mitchel became apprentice to the Guardian. He was chosen not through the usual trials—as that would have exposed the Altoriae, who was not ready for the Realm to know her name—but by personal choice. I needed someone who was unfailingly on Shari's side, and that's exactly what he was.

Training proved that while he was adept at many forms of hnarn, growing things back to size was not amongst them. **Dying was.**

Samuel! You can't write things like that in the Handbook! **Just did** *Samuel. Sorry Shari.*

Mitchel leaves behind his father, Daniel Hoffman, and his siblings, Jana, Kris, Krya, and Lyndal.

Mortimer Heath-Ribeck

Of Ronah.

Mu

Currently of Ronah. Formerly of Nindonia. Plasma Innarnian. Former candidate for the Guardian's Apprentice. Member of the Altoriae's Guild.

Muran Curtis

Formerly of Ronah. The sixth Altoriae. He lived until he was 45 years old and was eaten by Anriluka. One of the Returned, and the Risen.

In my defence, I was saving Jonathan. He's surprisingly unaware of his surroundings. Muran, though, will just not stay dead. At least he doesn't seem to hate me for killing him. Death by fitri can't be pleasant.

N

Natalie Ribeck

Of Ronah. Head Healer.

Neeth

Of Talhan. One of the patrol leaders.

Neev

Guardian of the ninth Altoriae.

Nerina

Of Ronah. Formally of the U'sala. Healer.

O

Oakley

Of Ginorti. Ginorti's Linked.

Octavia Young

Of Ronah. Joined the Guardian's patrol to Lefo in 4049.

Orla

Of Cantash. Formerly of Talhan. One of Eva's crew.

P

Pala

Leader of the Ducibus and sentinel of Lissae's gateway.

Peadar

Of Lissae. Patrol Leader who watched Larrian be brought back to life by the technomancer.

Petuar

The second Altoriae. She lived until she was 1005 years old when an accident caused her death.

Q

Qar

Guardian of the third Altoriae.

Q'Aralide

Of Ronah. The remains of a once feared race are now found on Carilla. See the next page for an image of the final family.

Lissae Series

R

RainbowMist

Deceased wife of SilverCloud, mother of Calem and Wolf Dawn.

Rany Thorne

Of Ronah. Father of Anika Thorne. *And a perfect example of how not to treat your hatchlings.*

Rashi

Of Lissae. A ship's captain. Mentor and friend of Talofa.

Raven

Currently of Ronah. Formerly of Freeson. Former candidate for the Guardian's Apprentice. New member of the Altoriae's Guild. Excellent tracker.

Reah

Of Cantash. Formerly of Talhan. One of Eva's crew. Recently lost her sight.

Reanna McMullin

Of Ronah. Looks after the horses. Joined the Guardian's patrol to Lefo in 4049. Victim of Anriluka and one of the Returned.

Remmy

Of Ronah. One of the Returned.

Resa Sunab

Guardian of Fiona MacAde, the twelfth Altoriae.

Rowan

Childhood friend of Alistair Hollingsworth. Killed by Jarnah wasps.

S

Samuel Caragnton

Currently of Ronah. Formerly of Altum. Golden Priest of the Q'Aralide turned Lissaen apprentice to the Guardian, *turned ritenberry farmer and elder?*

Born out of an illicit alliance to a mad queen, I am thankfully the only Q'Aralide to be able to shapeshift. Mentored by Izarrk on how to handle both the elders and the Realms, I was set free just after I gained my colours and ordered to survey the Realms. The sights I saw were all overtain with the knowledge that the mad queen could use them for evil. Guess I don't have to worry about her anymore.

Once the most feared being on the Realms, I have found a home, a family, friends, and a purpose that involves something other than maiming, killing, and torture. For that, I will be ever thankful.

A final note of warning: if you even think of harming me or mine, you won't have to worry about your life for very long.

Sanithane

See **Samuel Caragnton**.

Sarina 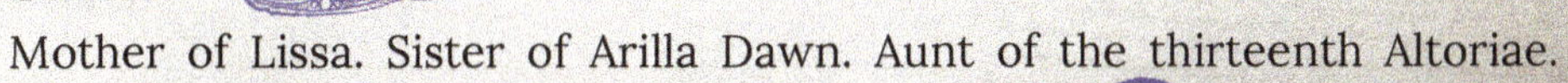

Mother of Lissa. Sister of Arilla Dawn. Aunt of the thirteenth Altoriae. Attacked by the Xanderri in 4045. Deceased.

Sean

Of Ronah. Brother of Kieran. One of the Returned.

Sebastian Silverstone

Of Ronah. Joined the Guardian's patrol to Lefo in 4049.

Serena

Of Ronah. Good at weapons maintenance.

Shael Robertson

The eight Altoriae. She lived until she was 73 years old, when an accident caused her death.

Shamus

Of Ronah. Patrolled with Edward and Jonathan Buan (who was an apprentice at the time). They were intercepted by a Q'Aralide.

Shamus still tells tales of how the now Guardian defeated one of the most terrifying beings of all time.

This does not need to be in the Handbook, Shari.

Oh, but it does.

I'm not that scary

I agree.

Shania

Of Ronah. Kay'imi's sister. Mother of Hensey.

Shari Dawn

Of Ronah. The thirteenth Altoriae of Lissae and creator of the Altoriae's Guild.

Shari became the Altoriae at only 3 years of age, after her mother suffered an attack right outside the gateway to Lissae. After years of training by herself, she finally found her Guardian.

You don't have to word it quite like that, Jonathan.

I can be blunter, if you like? Carry on.

At 17 years old, Shari underwent rigorous testing to prove to the elders that Lissae had indeed chosen the strongest hnarnian as her Altoriae. Shari passed with flying colours and minimal loss of life.

Do you know how odd it is to read about yourself in a book, knowing that future Altoriaes will pull your life apart to see where you went wrong?

Shari Dawn is not what I was expecting. She is quite possibly the toughest being in all the Realms. I much prefer when she is safe. Home. And mostly intact.

She has to be the most stubborn, infuriating being on all the Realms, yet I would burn everything to ash for her.

I will forever be grateful that she is free to make her own choices, at last.

SilverCloud

Of Rakemyst. Father of Calem and Wolf Dawn. Husband of RainbowMist. Grandfather of the thirteenth Altoriae. Head Elder of Rakemyst. Deceased.

Skye

Currently visiting Talhan. Former Aide to Elder **Suni**. Helper for **Grace**.

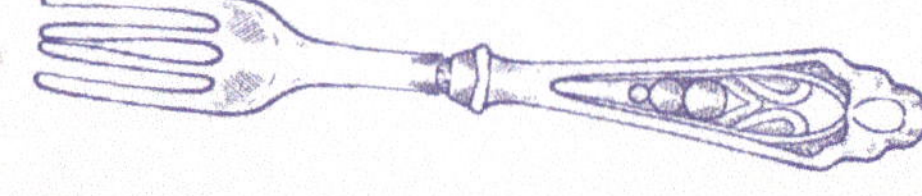

Sorsha Hollingsworth

Of Lissae. Estranged sister of Alistair and Christopher Hollingsworth.

Sulak

Of the Da'mar. Former candidate for the Guardian's Apprentice.

Suni

Of Lawrgaea. Elder. Falsely accused of being an Innarnian and summarily executed whilst she slept. Deceased.

T

Tabatha

Guardian of Abby Thorne, the eleventh Altoriae.

Talofa

Currently of Ronah. Formerly of Sulanta. Former candidate for the Guardian's Apprentice. Member of the Altoriae's Guild.

Tania Hollingsworth

Of Ronah. Ronah's Linked. Daughter of Liza, stepdaughter of Jordan. Sister to Caleb, Christopher, Alistair, and Jessica.

Tania was another Innarnian late to discover her abilities. It was only after her family moved to Ronah and she wanted to ask the mayor about how her new house had been designed that she discovered she could hear the Shifting Island she now called home.

Adept at Earth, Air, and Water Innarn, and learning more about Crystal Innarn from the technomancer and Talhan's Linked, Tania has been banned from leaving Ronah due to the weakening of her Link when off-Realm.

Another friend. Just how many do I have? I still can't figure out why all these mortals want me as their friend. I used to be the most feared being in all the Realms.

Tanika Riley

The seventh Altoriae. She lived until she was 46 years old. The only Altoriae to die via natural causes.

Temira

Of Talhan. Formerly of **Ulnan.** Also called the technomancer, Temira is Head Healer and head of the Techno Centre. *My apologies for the destruction of your Realm. It was not (entirely) my fault. My race is... horrid. And possibly no more—if that's any comfort. Whilst apologies for the destruction of your race are overdue, I didn't think stabbing you is going to help any. May Cyfanthar guide your soul.*

Terrance Thorne

Of Ronah. Saved from disembowelment by the Guardian. Anika Thorne's uncle. *Waste of space. Ugh. This one. Stay dead already!*

Therdon

Of Rakemyst. Former candidate for the Guardian's Apprentice. Killed by the thirteenth Altoriae for tampering with the minds of others.

Therion

Of Jinkor. Part of the mainlanders' troops.

Thuk

Guardian of the second Altoriae. One of the Risen.

Tim

Of Lissae. Ships boy at the same time as Jonathan Buan.

Timon

Of Ronah. Innarnian Architect. One of the Returned.

Timony

Of Talhan. Assistant to **Fortesque**, the Travel Innarnian.

Titch

Of Cantash. Draci keeper who works in the Gardens.

Tobias

Of Ronah. Son of Joana. One of the Returned. Also known as Toby. Deceased due to experimentation by Chamele.

Tommie

Of Lissae. Sailor and mainlander sent to assassinate the Altoriae. Banished to the mainland by Guardian Buan.

Torden Dealon

Of Ronah. Formerly of Canak-Maku. One of the Returned, and a member of the Altoriae's Guild.

Tormorylth

Of ~~Altom~~. *Ronah. Q'Avalide hatchling who gained her colours and terrorises her elders.*

Trainor

Of Talhan. One of Elder SilverCloud's guards.

Tutor Boyce

Of Ronah. Maths teacher at Ridden Hall.

Tutor Heath-Ribeck

Of Ronah. Science teacher at Ridden Hall.

U

Uista Zeypher

Of Ronah. Joined the Guardian's patrol to Lefo in 4049.

Ullmar

Guardian of the fourth Altoriae. One of the Risen.

U'sala

A group of beings from all over the Realms who have banded together to protect the Realms from creatures who wish to change them for their own benefit. Currently led by Yessna. The numbers of the U'sala vary because of the high turnover rate.

V

Varlee

Of Rakemyst. Third in command of Elder SilverCloud's guards. One of the patrol members in Wolf's group. Spouse of Charin.

Varox

Fallen member of the U'sala. Killed by the Chirea.

Voxis

Of Rakemyst. Silver-winged Ilutri youth. Nephew of Zana, Linked of Rakemyst.

Vren

Of Talhan. Head of Vitreus Academy.

W

Wellik

Of Lissae. He watched his friend, Larrian, be brought back to life by the technomancer.

Whitmore

Formerly of Ioyitmar. An elder, and a Water Innarnian.

Wolf Dawn

Of Rakemyst. Mate of **Belfar**. Brother of **Calem Dawn**, and uncle to the thirteenth Altoriae. Former commander of **SilverCloud**'s guards. Previously known as **LoneWolf Dawn**.

Wren

Of Freeson. Brother to Raven.

Wubi

Of the **U'sala**. Wielder of the spiked chain.

X

Xani

Of Talhan. Also called the technomancer, Xani is Head Healer and head of the Techno Centre. Due to injuries, she rides in a hovering, crystal-powered chair and doesn't speak. One of the Risen - without any of her former injuries.

Y

Yessna

Of the U'sala. Second in command. *Pain in my scales. Don't trust anything the Ferah has to say about me. She's biased.*

Yirri

Refugee now living on Ronah. Mother of Yirrisaunder.

Yirrisaunder

Refugee living on Ronah. Son of Yirri.

Yvonne

Of Ginorti. Part of the Satyrs' army.

Z

Zac Hudson

Of Talhan. Formerly of Ronah. Techno apprentice. *Shari says they don't need permission to become intimate with each other? How do two males make hatchlings, anyway? Samuel, that info isn't appropriate for the Handbook. Come and see me. Ah. Well. If anyone can put up with Jonathan, it's Zac.*

Zali

Of Cantash. Formerly of Talhan. One of Eva's crew.

Zana

Of Rakemyst. Rakemyst's Linked. Eldest of the Linked, she is an accomplished diplomat.

Zana has the unique ability to see soul-matches due to meeting her match in her youth, only to lose her to an unfortunate incident off-Realm.

Often taking the role of advisor to the other Linked, Zana does her best not to enforce Rakemyst's stuffy version of help onto the other Shifting Islands, as he does not believe his occupants need to fight in order for Lissae to flourish.

Zodian Doonavan

Of Ronah. Joined the Guardian's patrol to Lefo in 4049.

Other Realms

Planets which inhabit various parts of the multiverse on three main levels: Dark, Grey, and Light. There are three main bands for each level, as well as many sub-levels per band.

Light realms are places where there is an abundance of natural light.

Grey Realms are places with a similar amount of light to Lissae and Earth's equator.

Dark Realms are places with little to no natural sunlight. Most lights in these Realms are made by Innarn.

Here is a place to record all the things you learn from around the realms. Ensure you are as detailed as possible, as it might help to save a life.

So much information is gone due to one fool who lost his fingers. Best of luck piecing the missing bits back together, little Altoriae. I fear that you are going to need it.

Map of the Light Realms
First Band

Sub-levels					
1	Binvie	Tisnosh	Pharban	Yilhil	Solium
2	Manohnon	Lathol	Fluck	Torene	Bolsover
3	Nimsath	Kalphie	Jacunor	Hanvirea	Selvan
4	Shatoh	Galzuds	Oberoth	Harsings	Mulosia
5	First Realm of Hell	Crotaz	Iozea		Utosmar
6	Vuchy	Dhestaid	Letovi	Sappain	Ahana
7	Firash	Hasions	Alolyne	Reasaita	Braetos
8	Rashnom	Buvi	Irrutha	Gloquio	Genne
9	Camelot	Dirruth	Ceobram	Tamutha	Lyniot

Map of the Light Realms
First Band

						Sub-levels
Zuefie	Althur	Tolves	Yattamunif	Xalthafsh	Fumish	1
Brisin	Gwynuvr	Nufsai	Raedru	Weaterra	Hiadore	2
Shiovion	Clotpe	Huadell	Paradupia	Voiarch	Quisn	3
Fioon	Diso	Wiaclo	Crujii	Dorweau	Flipendell	4
Pioron	Renastan	Monest	Huath	Ruriped	Urtha	5
Kelton	Scettan	Ioyitmar	Slellivion	Jurin	Rodellen	6
Livghar	Zelbon	Neacia	Curthua	Egraia	Moltran	7
Otha	Rugrllihar	Griagha	Sonneacia	Gharhen	Lemus	8
Jinet	Elerain	Seappion	Rastlyn	Moiam	Neatope	9

Map of the Light Realms
Second Band

Sub-levels					
1	Yehhora	Palaski	Vestil	Nerubia	Qash
2	Inadin	Slevania	Zajiphere	Osindell	Gonarath
3	Peonara	Cioathane	Xomika	Gif	Rikotara
4	Fluothra	Dawoxus	Misleiwese	Behl	Boepens
5	Second Realm of Hell	Fuppethan	Uzatika	Tande	Ehiaranah
6	Easetara	Keahos	Ozajan	Ulfan	Ferodalon
7	Gal'terah	Hospea	Ninnphere	Fanethra	Scanxous
8	Kiondin	Yaretzi	Lionnat	Raeonara	Iogasnae
9	Wrikoran	Flachaeus	Jeastika	Vatanonath	Aovania

Map of the Light Realms
Second Band

						Sub-levels
Pebbead	Sememer	Nosaven	Feabalar	Rhorle	Zumaynn	1
Abaium	Dunharrow	Veamar	Glexlar	Phessamos	Shaefoe	2
Bazaven	Raqeege	Uonium	Orna	Riadiria	Kever	3
Zothas	Celestonia	Adyar	Welft	Iabalarh	Giokk	4
Eonner	Qemear	Menium	Kerina	Ssanass	Yaggtis	5
Hikuban	Prioeon	Coatl	Unonde	Tomiod	Phusitha	6
Leakati	Guckarion	Therrala	Jioyux	Joria	Shiojas	7
Murerion	Oggetis	Zioyal	Diaven	Kiodax	Rynn	8
Xarion	Natizu	Xatiar	Sowriad	Laekk	Varshae	9

Map of the Light Realms
Third Band

<table>
<tr><td rowspan="9">Sub-levels</td><td>1</td><td>Huluoxant</td><td>Piamos</td><td>Iadesan</td><td>Ventatar</td><td>Menonary</td></tr>
<tr><td>2</td><td>Abriea</td><td>Nahuatl</td><td>Xiaynew</td><td>Tiomode</td><td>Topexus</td></tr>
<tr><td>3</td><td>Eteonary</td><td>Qowianem</td><td>Fluzus</td><td>Keroria</td><td>Crihimos</td></tr>
<tr><td>4</td><td>Feepian</td><td>Werath</td><td>Citlalli</td><td>Worg</td><td>Neahrath</td></tr>
<tr><td>5</td><td>Third Realm of Hell</td><td>Muzzan</td><td>Deeth</td><td>Caltiaus</td><td>Geteopia</td></tr>
<tr><td>6</td><td>Jellarat</td><td>Byranthia</td><td>Nexatrope</td><td>Mioboxus</td><td>Hiaymon</td></tr>
<tr><td>7</td><td>Owelar</td><td>Zering</td><td>Heroria</td><td>Channoum</td><td>Duhiomel</td></tr>
<tr><td>8</td><td>Riateon</td><td>Uiamolar</td><td>Heamaron</td><td>Aquasands</td><td>Lusinea</td></tr>
<tr><td>9</td><td>Stogel</td><td>Wiaxatale</td><td>Lioccanor</td><td>Yumbaland</td><td>Kiayiamos</td></tr>
</table>

Map of the Light Realms
Third Band

						Sub-levels
The Hallowed	Janacre	Fintae	Bslian	Caedivrae	Larblath	1
Doqonot	Acidigeth	Handop	Reaeg	Axghion	Klaxira	2
Gartum	Gipjoth	Shiorhia	Vionlar	Qaroon	Ninale	3
Fenaxor	Ritejan	Orver	Meojuary	Ronet	Sileox	4
Iippopp	Craeope	Praxore	Rathgar	Sibbigh	Peoira	5
Peojan	Ellevar	Duppria	Sliaur	Mafay	Gleorxi	6
Uanor	Muppina	Jerohia	Xau	Vedalar	Jaxenor	7
Glever	Oarth	Taeglev	Lommnet	Vancinit	Netoque	8
Tocithas	Hoggeotis	Neviarath	Parrlet	Baranonet	Ciddig	9

Map of the Grey Realms
First Band

Sub-levels					
1	Colrin	Tatium	Bentrom	Francole	Aebram
2	Alfraosu	Dasyatis	Reillo	Almegmen	Yinsi
3	Enshobos	Molmun	Bastienn	Shu'hru'ear	Lerolod
4	Numnuco	Ginzandas	Zabbonsun	Yognue	Petrichor
5	Fourth Realm of Hell	Shomdegu	Gerringoth	Zylvie	Hamder
6	Mogyiem	Rangao	Canticum	Saapienn	Canak
7	Vunlon	Pasler	Flumenn	Liaton	Suttporia
8	Dostubbe	Myliobat	Lunae	Shiells	Felsun
9	Samdecol	Ogged	Alē	Zualfriegae	Rummi

Map of the Grey Realms
First Band

Paxivon	Emorson	Candr	Rainyln	Briylan	Zaick	1
Atlantis	Goazon	Webne	Aolnem	Runbur	Ternce	2
Reznofid	Belfrom	Massay World	Begnebun	Yunthala	Faelinest	3
Muble	Yonup	Liesaem	Tasnzar	Dummusan	Naayaan	4
Gerhar	Middle Earra	Elfrao	Yenudon	Tuziev	Haerlo	5
Zokleran	Zomun	Velthorn	Shuslar	Uhlueh	Kasivon	6
Aopel	Renge	Xallogar	Upper Bantaris	Damya	Bhenna	7
Hunthage	Ionnan	Dilno	Nages	Wamius	Aliegh	8
Jaggongud	Kunthfuo	Qugoatia	Asdugno	Obdun	Shasdy	9

Sub-levels

Map of the Grey Realms
Second Band

Sub-levels					
1	Doznuts	Thunsod	Zunhum	Xalbiuvoa	Yobnues
2	Qonie	Bacopa	Amdu	Gubda	Mid Shunar
3	Xteria	Nenzo	Pet'hur	Shun'hur	Nindunrus
4	Hushun	Lisud	Beneebun	Ponton	Earra
5	Fifth Realm of Hell	Piltarn	Iabovar	Zylvabranc	Mid Lissae
6	Nonthuan	Bonylis	Iskryn	Aubbun	Daixam
7	Vannul	Monnafan	Ineru	Nanka-Canak	Lenouu
8	Somdu	Gaagturu	Bomaduar	Nanka	Ezles
9	Xelss	Rihenze	Yugnuam	Zazzlen	Nemiasta

Map of the Grey Realms
Second Band

							Sub-levels
Lamink	Nalluanz	Zaamnal	Roblues	Gumles	Xanlange		1
La'sua	Dansua	Mid Dansua	Sontela	Hahnenur	Melzorian		2
Onie	World	Nebius	Nuntes	Kaelith	Wualbuas		3
Earth	Terra Massay	Mid Massay	Massay	Nebius	Ficent		4
Lissae	Libertatia	Osgood	Neharn	Asylum	Carilla		5
Mid Canak	Weavers Realm	Malum Piscium	Statumort	Seblefo	Hunedao		6
Bahus	Sognob	Lovofen	Bantaris	Connor	Toummo		7
Lower Maru	Amaer	Gooslun	Karara	Guzell	Hiblolam		8
Caszuve	Enyu	Robbohor	Xaviour	Hawam	Bislossah		9

Map of the Grey Realms
Third Band

1	Grunyin	Stargonia	Famlur	Auha	Muhoostu
2	Oggehur	Tuklopia	Nuastis	Qubao	Shunar
3	Zaostuld	Emdocan	Gakodia	Xniem	Onala
4	Stalduos	Kshoolur	Ohnovo	Zubbul	Eraldreach
5	Sixth Realm of Hell	Malum	Piscium	Teeldrit	Vinneča
6	Lendrol	Urymith	Stuggea	Nulburu	Xabbul
7	Balud	Junluad	Wonovao	Bahnassad	Canak-Maku
8	Zusele	Ilgehur	Permian	Vunni	Guhma
9	Costendrol	Duoscan	Rabelde	Fiotealar	Hilbrondres

Sub-levels

Map of the Grey Realms
Third Band

						Sub-levels
Yubu	Nulburu	Malenzou	Zunthendor	Bahnassad	Oslu	1
La'suawrl	Wegon	Anle	Shagiade	Shorage	Nassega	2
Kilgaroth	Bublada	Senagoul	Nasobber	Xolnholm	Buludro	3
Lower Earth	Subdo	Umahar	Sahyezal	Yhaled	Tegabahn	4
Riomache	Greon	Fueshal	Behshou	Luerix	Sugtega	5
Folnus	Yahlom	Halfrobeh	Frobbeh	Laahal	Xigu	6
Maru	Amer-Maru	Shousahou	Nittany	Ranuel	Yebbem	7
Henshal	Gegihfo	Rilite	Sonthan	Thandir	Gulies	8
Vutolea	Analanzu	Ongegish	Kebbem	Jommue	Lomdo	9

Map of the Dark Realms
First Band

Sub-levels					
1	Manddon	Imvoho	Myrelum	Saelmi	Rezusyt
2	Lamendue	Tesynric	Danorin	Wuzondec	Narlido
3	Nyamu	Knasari	Zisadain	Aikze	Coqi
4	Qondelphi	Fumance	Reben	Bamryn	Gilusca
5	Seventh Realm of Hell	Thakhane	Khanebrass	Obrassius	Herlcum
6	Menthea-Thakhane	Menthea	Theakane	Ossebu	Vosuvron
7	Gulkothea	Thakhane-Menthea	Jaem	Krozur	Pulrome
8	Yeligulko	Lefo	Duhlisi	Camade	Theigneth
9	Fezelo	Thosana	Nombalo	Enrel	Lipidra

Map of the Dark Realms
First Band

						Sub-levels
Gharithurih	Theirzus	Elviebiu		Phrivar		1
Pehndoth	Gimopop	Ralera	Chilrok	Kosanvri	Voluchal	2
Warvumod	Bacruss	Bimrumi	Tisruc	Chalvolu	Sheriorth	3
Dhesria	Rilzilo	Sherziduc	Karinom	Yhiemas	Gaizard	4
Teroupi	Ratou	Viondikh	~~ULNAN~~	Ieshro	Zardrath	5
Khivril	Gerius	Simaegus	Shulmar	Kimeir	Fairnuth	6
Viorath	Qidremi	Phandebu	Degnamit	Gimorsi	Jusarack	7
Bhovren	Cirsir	Gytraedh	Thisrune	Mirdra	Xinuth	8
Ridogun	Nadny	Niugrad	Chelehe	Hunudva	Qiemnu	9

Map of the Dark Realms
Second Band

Sub-levels					
1	Gaerro	Theti	Lwazisa	Banvrugosh	Zoknuk
2	Cilei	Fumeli	Bolwai	Dhupecni	Cailvieh
3	Bayo	Tezeli	Masei	Qalfyd	Ghuzosrast
4	Dethaethro	Xolula	Lulailan	Yudo	Quixhefp
5	Eighth Realm of Hell	Recurox	Curoxlai	Nukzok	Hadfro
6	Lelmaro	Oraemedi	Meddila	Dilaphix	Tostrat
7	Haerox	Salubin	Binond	Ondpho	Vomdre
8	Eofix	Ilrime	Lehond	Phoziu	Yrusri
9	Dayox	Fibys	Honys	Nysiu	Zathakled

Map of the Dark Realms
Second Band

Cycmykh	Gacenda	Aecle	Ikros	Navriamo	Iunder		1
Nozeldrut	Phalrar	Rhanibur	Varviac	Pezium	Dovriat		2
Thankled	Orduth	Ehalrah	Zamdric	Tegnaba	Rugnen		3
Druvnol	Mahemri	Hacenda	Pumbakin	Kopica	Zeibesh		4
Vomdre	Tholzubaeh	Idvemu	Wacenda	Dhanro	Ghopul	Sub-levels	5
Shunnie	Malreth	Liraruth	~~RAVAL~~	Xerduth	Cubsisu		6
Rordruch	Brudrin	Qurozresh	Urbaeh	Krustos	Adruii		7
Ueanu	Japtukk	Cradamull	Gapauho	Nemogath	Zoiban		8
Rataeo	Ponut	Findas	~~MISHONE~~	Jaemish	Yezesh		9

Map of the Dark Realms
Third Band

Sub-levels					
1	Falita	Kisfier	Rohfall	Volhuss	Nalbba
2	Aimuth	Twethunn	Oilla	Qewa	Tosandei
3	Muthuku	Juiqao	Cukogh	Huica	Phtonis
4	Xuhfenn	Benihu	Nawzin	Tuposhu	Drilmanu
5	Ninth Realm of Hell	Vennph	Vastilda	Baenge	Tiaclorune
6	Loughaden	Jacuinnond	Ewalfoea	Nibzoll	Vikthasi
7	Xuaroi	Drubaic	Kintage	Cuplith	Woicull
8	Ginsoeh	Rarix	Oenthe	Roefill	Zooghe
9	Zipthide	Hasend	Morreth	Ukkcew	Poema

Map of the Dark Realms
Third Band

						Sub-levels
Yaponque	Atuten	Risuexe	Gordeli	Illoveth	Lotsmilner	1
Saundun	Eai	Bopeth	Locfog	Basaun	Closphal	2
Wosnuqui	Fumtull	Muzeh	Helfish	Kaddell	Yhomtill	3
Yettara	Strozna	Gebaniu	Urpanra	Shino	Zaccuinde	4
Gihalan	Dakleozen	Hinioxar	Panagar	Eazithan	Obirim	5
Fasleix	Iosa	Oemeeth	Cawaxe	Neokgli	Temtha	6
Juhis	Yilush	Kiegie	Frocra	Uzkoat	Mohcall	7
Agueshi	Damiuth	Dreugui	Sisgor	Otike	Aepollo	8
Altum	Eunzem	Fleggei	Hersuiun	Pudbiho	Wetfithee	9

Ducibus' Hall

The place between Realms, guarded by the **Ducibus**. The Portal ensures beings from all over can travel safely between places. Intricately layered Innarn safeguards mean that each traveller sees only members of their own party and not others who are also travelling.

Also referred to as the **Portal**.

Beings and Creatures

Ducibus

Sentinels of the gateways, Ducibus come from all the beings across the Realms. No one really knows what they look like, as they all wear dark cloaks. They ensure safe travel between Realms and that those who aren't meant to get through, don't.

Ellora

Of the Ducibus. Sentinel of the Suttporia Gateway. Friend of Mitchel.

Mitchel

Of the Ducibus. Formerly of Ronah and known as el (Mitch) Hoffman. Sentinel of Carilla's gateway.

Pala

Leader of the Ducibus and sentinel of Lissae's gateway.

Sulpa

Of the Ducibus. Former sentinel of the Ulnan gateway. Gave their life to protect the Ulanians.

Mother Realm

The only Realm capable of giving birth to new Realms. Highly guarded and sought after.

Neutral Realm

A Realm where Innarn is impossible.

Nine Hells

The name given to a particularly nasty set of nine Realms. The first three Hells are in the Light Realms, the mid three (Hells Four, Five, and Six) are in the Grey Realms, and the last three are in the Dark Realms.

Pocket Realm

A small Realm that is attached to a larger one.

Portal

The place between Realms, guarded by the **Ducibus**. Also referred to as the **Ducibus' Hall**.

Spirit Realm

A Realm that is found alongside Lissae, where the spirit or souls of the deceased go when their physical bodies are no longer needed.

BEINGS AND CREATURES FROM ACROSS THE REALMS

A list of beings found across the Realms, where their home is not defined.

Cyclops

This is the common term for a being with one eye. Usually found with two legs and two arms, Cyclops are native to many Realms. Variants in skin tone and number of limbs may help to indicate the Realm of origin.

Fehar

Humanoid beings with cat-like features—including fur, a tail, whiskers, and claws—they mostly reside in the Grey and Dark Realms. They possess quite a few unique features, including a third and fourth set of eyelids. The third eyelid protects them from dust and other elements, where the fourth set allows them to read a being's aura.

Fehar stand between 4 feet and 7 feet tall, with prehensile tails that are usually as long as their legs. Covered in fur and possessing paws with elongated fingers, they have cat-like ears and the acute hearing—as well as other extraordinary senses—to go along with them.

Fehar are telepathic and can use some minor, usually elementary magic. They rely on instincts more than on their Innarn.

Shadow Bringer

Sent to watch over others, sometimes to protect, often to kill.

WORDS FROM ACROSS THE REALMS

Alphabet of the Dark Realms

A	B	C	D	E	F	G

H	I	J	K	L	M	N

O	P	Q	R	S	T	U

V	W	X	Y	Z	,	.

Curses

Curses from the Realms include:

ketarr	dathae	tu'zar
tongue of a Ne'fora	whale's ass	cestoray
slime vattar	hanotqe	slime-filled cedore
feseor	gozochas	thrice-damned
fizzpot	trusnuck	blyknot
basalt-chewing hemmit-loving buzzard		

Dark Conclave

Less likely to work together than the others, the Dark Realms still have their own overarching council. The meeting minutes of the Conclave are recorded in the Hekkor Mafae.

Doublespeak

A dauntless, dangerous task undertaken when trying to stay alive.

Gateways

The name for the access point to and from a Realm. Typically appears as a doorway. The Ducibus' Hall contains one side of each entry point—the other being on the Realm it leads to.

Grytycide

A deadly poison with only two cures—removing it from the victim's system or ingesting Dudrodie eggs.

Hekkor Mafae

A book so imbued with Dark Innarn that it is painful for anyone from the Grey or Light Realms to even be around the tome. It contains tales from the Dark Realms and the meeting minutes of the Dark Conclave.

Konraei

A promise which must be upheld, or your life becomes forfeit.

Prime

Non-binary equivalent of prince or princess.

Xarits

Special portals which enable travel to and from neighbouring Realms. There are only a handful of Realms that have xarits leading to them. Only one side of the xarit is a Realm where Innarn is possible, the other side is completely neutral.

Light Realms

Ahana

A Light Realm of the first band.

Beings and Creatures

Ahana

The Ahana are from a Light Realm, but not much more is known about them. A lone Innarnian Ahana archer is credited with the death of Kay'imi. Said to be from the very Light Realms, the Ahana have faded into history.

Bazaven

A Light desert Realm of the second band. Native beings include the **Sylpans** (See: Sylpan) and the **Ofanahni** (See: Ofanahni).

Beings and Creatures

Ofanahni

Native to Bazaven. The Ofanahni are typically oppressed by the Sylpans, whose brutal and inconsistent justice system makes their lives difficult. A group of Ofanahni refugees has settled in the desert region of the continent set aside on Lissae for refugees.

Sylpan

A double-headed being native to Bazaven, who hunts and imprisons those they consider to have "done them wrong". What is wrong to a Sylpan depends on the day and hour, but if they feel slighted at all, they will hunt you to the end of the Realm to bring you to justice.

Crihimos

A Light Realm of the third band. A day's walk from the gateway are ruins of what must have once been a great town.

Duhiomel

A Light Realm of the third band, home to a variant of cyclops. The **Sivertrie Woods** guard the gateway off-Realm. In the Ducibus' hallway, Duhiomel is accessed through a carved door with an intricate leaf pattern. The door opens directly into a creek bed.

Places

Sivertrie Woods
These woods guard the gateway to Duhiomel.

Ellevar

A Light Realm of the third band.

Flachaeus

A Light Realm of the second band.

Beings and Creatures

Ekrix
Native to Flachaeus, the ekrix is a small, plant-eating lizard with a poisonous bite.

Hoggeotis

A Light Realm of the third band, with traps around the gateway.

Ioyitmar

A Light desert Realm of the first band. Some refugees found their way from here to Lissae after civil unrest.

Lioccanor

A Light Realm of the third band.

Beings and Creatures

Iomnuroz

A creature with razor-sharp claws.

I came across a herd of Iomnuroz while patrolling. They startle easily, and their hides seem to be immune to Innarn. It is strongly suggested that you do not get in the way of their claws, as the marks they leave tend to scar.

Side note: I need to work on my glamour more, as one of the creatures swiped at me. I don't blame it, but by Lissae, it stings worse than expected. Why are there so many nerves in your face?

Mafay

A Light Realm of the third band that is home to fire-breathing dragons.

Beings and Creatures

Fire-breathing dragons

No one has been game enough to get close and find out what they call themselves.

Plants

Thorny vines

Prone to tearing skin and material alike, these vines are the perfect protection as nothing in the Realms wants to go near them.

Meojuary

A Light Realm of the third band.

Neviarath

A Light Realm of the third band with particularly nasty bugs invading the jungle near the gateway.

Orna

A Light Realm of the second band.

Beings and Creatures

Ornaians

Satyrs with furry legs and cloven feet.

Hemmin Bane

A Plasma Innarnian. A diplomat during the 4047 expedition to Lissae. *Holds the dubious title of First to attempt assassinating Jonathan Buan.* Samuel!

Rulla Woth

A diplomat during the 4047 expedition to Lissae.

Vallen Lowe

A Spirit Innarnian. Lead Diplomat during the 4047 expedition to Lissae.

Food and Drink

Ornaian wine

Famous across the Realms, the wine is made from grapes sweetened with nectar only available on Orna. Rich and sweet, *it is also the perfect drink to disguise poison in.* How did you even hear about this? *I have my sources.*

Items

Venbarium poison

The weapon of choice used during the 4047 diplomatic expedition to Lissae in an attempt to kill Guardian Buan.

Praxore

A Light Realm of the third band on the Lissaen patrol schedule.

Shiovion

A Light Realm of the first band.

Beings and Creatures

Shiovionian

A being from Shiovion.

Lord Telnarik

Leader of the Sentinel Division. Possessed and then murdered by the Xanderri.

Tocithas

A Light water Realm of the third band. The local population are likely to spear first and ask questions later.

The majority of the Realm is underwater, which suits the residents, as they have perfectly adapted to the conditions.

When travelling to Tocithas, make sure your Air Innarn is strong enough to pull the correct amount of oxygen directly into your lungs. If not—avoid.

Beings and Creatures

Aestques
Beings native to Tocithas.

Lakin, Prime
Prime Lakin is second in line to the Throne of Startide and ruling the people of Tocithas.

Throne of Startide
The leader of the Realm holds a position called the Throne of Startide. This is akin to the Altoriae but focuses primarily on protecting Tocithas rather than patrolling other Realms.

Zarsuth
Ancient aquatic fish native to Tocithas.

Places

Startide
The capital city of Tocithas and home to their ruling family.

Wiaxatale

A Light Realm of the third band whose gateway into Lissae is currently under external attack.

Zelbon

A Light Realm of the first band which almost saw the untimely demise of Guardian Buan of Lissae, due to a tripwire placed at waist height.

Zuefie

A Light Realm of the first band.

Avoid. Just don't even touch the gateway. Zuefie should not be entered under any circumstances. Nothing should be allowed in or out of the Realm.

Beings and Creatures

Xanderri

A cloud-like race relying on the bodies of their hosts to move between Realms. As they feed on Innarn, the Xanderri have been banned from the Portal by the Ducibus.

Derri

Sister of Xan. Co-founder of the Xanderri.

Xan

Brother of Derri. Co-founder of the Xanderri.

GREY REALMS

Amaer

A Grey desert Realm of the second band. Dry, desolate, and rocky, the landscape has been altered by the kemmae. In 4049, there was an infestation of pteradiles which was cleared by the Q'Aralide.

Atlantis

A Grey Realm of the first band with a predominantly human population, it is famous for its Techno Innarn and wide variety of Innarn-powered machines. We just don't ask where they got the Innarn from.

Beings and Creatures

Atlantians
The name of the beings of Atlantis.

Archer Terion
Of Atlantis. Merlyn Terion's Husband. Donated his brain to one of Nisethran's experiments and woke up as someone else. See **Asterion**.

Merlyn
Of Atlantis, Archer Terion's wife. Accidentally killed by Archer.

Nisethran
Of Atlantis. Mad scientist and successful myth creator.

Oitane
Of Atlantis. Diplomat. *She's as much of a diplomat as Shari is.*

Places

Meropis

Capital city of the Realm of Atlantis.

Penemiota Wilds

Jungle between Meropis and the gateway on the Realm of Atlantis.

Technology

Skipstep

A clear disc used for Shifting from one place to another on Atlantis.

Medical Mythology Program

Created by Nisethran, the MMP is a way of giving mythology a new lease on life through modern medicine. Successful recreations include:

> The Minotaur
>
> The Kraken
>
> Hercules
>
> Controllable Lightning

The program was disbanded when it was discovered that Nisethran was using unwilling participants.

He... of all the beings in all the realms, I regret not causing Nisethran's death.

Sharil

You're just mad cause you want a stab at him too.

Bantaris

A Grey Realm of the second band.

Beings and Creatures

Kemmae

Originally from Bantaris, they are a race of malicious mischief-makers who delight in moulding the earth of the Realm they inhabit to make it inhospitable to others. They are crab-like in appearance, standing between two and four inches tall and between six and eight inches across; their pincers have a toxic coating which eats away at the flesh of humanoids.

Canak—Maku

A Grey Realm of the third band that is home to the minotaurs.

Beings and Creatures

Minotaur

Bull-headed bipedal beings, minotaurs live on the Realm of Canak—Maku. Generally a peaceful race, unless they are away from home and then they will fight to get back.

Carilla

New Grey Realm in the second band.

Sentinel

Mitchel

Of the Ducibus.

Dansua

A Grey Realm of the second band.

Daixam

A Grey Realm of the second band.

Beings and Creatures

Diaxampal

Refugees from the Grey Realm of **Daixam**, now living on Lissae. Many of the refugees were treated by the Technomancer for serious wounds before they were resettled.

Earra

A Grey Realm of the second band whose gateway comes out at the top of a cliff which overlooks a winding river fed from a glacier. Their major city sits on the opposite bank. A broad, paved platform indicates the inhabitants frequently travel across the Realms. Earra is aiming at taking Luerix over.

Beings and Creatures

Ruthford

of **Earra**. Tasked with guarding their side of the gateway.

Earth

A Grey Realm of the second band with ley lines like Lissae. Once the home of Atlantis before it split away to form its own Realm. Also home to the myth of the minotaur, and most of the readers of this series.

Places

Arctic Ocean

A place cold enough to be one of the Hells.

Eystribyggð

A frozen hellscape Light enough to burn my soul. Full of friends I never wished to harm.

Beings and Creatures

Cow

A large, multipurpose quadruped. Produces milk and meat.

Humans

The main population of beings on Earth.

Brigitta

Of Earth. Wife of Erik, mother to Lavran.

Erik

Of Earth. Husband of Brigitta, father to Lavran. *My first friend*

Hakon

Of Earth. On of the walrus hunters,

Huyenn

One of Odin's ravens.

King Magnus

Of Earth. Son of Princess Ingebjørg.

Lavran

Of Earth. Son of Brigitta and Erik.

Munenn

One of Odin's ravens.

Odin

Norse Deity. Has two jet black birds, Huyenn and Munenn.

Princess Ingebjørg

Of Earth. Due to marry. Mother of King Magnus.

Readers

Those who choose to believe in books and fantasy. The best kind of beings.

Roelof

Of Earth. Healer.

Sheep

A quadruped with a fluffy body. The fleece can be removed and used to make cloth.

Walrus

A sea creature hunted for ivory, blubber, hide, and meat.

Words and phrases

Dreki
Norse for Dragon.

Taufr
Norse for magician.

Fiotealar

A Grey Realm of the third band, known for its technological prowess. Home of the **Yoxant**. Their gateway is exceptionally well protected, and as such, the realm has been removed from the patrolling schedule.

Do Not Patrol!

Beings and Creatures

Yoxant

Beings native to **Fiotealar**. Incredibly gifted in techno Innarn, they are the creators of some of the most sought-after technology in the Grey Realms. The Yoxants are more than willing to fight to keep their technology out of the hands (or claws) of others. Their preferred weapon is the chakram.

Items

Chakram

A disk-like blade with a razor-sharp edge and a large hole in the centre. Only a few species use it as their preferred weapon. The Yoxant are one such species. Also listed under **Weapons: Chakram**

Amara lost her life trying to make sure this realm was safe from the various beings who would try to take it over.

No other patroller or member of the Altoriae's Guild is to step foot, claw or paw on this realm unless explicitly stated by Shari Dawn.

Gerhar

A Grey Realm of the first band that sits above Lissae and is one of the easiest Realms to get to.

Beings and Creatures

Ebb

A human farmer whom Shari meets while patrolling to see what the Chirea were destroying. *Potential ally.*

Sareglui

A creature standing at six feet tall, they have scaled hides come in bronze, copper and the occasional zirconium shade. Their sense of smell is unparalleled. Small slitted eyes mean the creature can't see at all, and they depend on the ropey whiskers around their nose to draw scents in. Despite being small, saregluis have excellent hearing. They are herbivores, and they coexist with the **vitampit**, who follow them around.

Vitampit

Small insects who travel in large swarms and deliver irritating, poisonous bites. Once a target is identified through a hive-mind, the swarm will seek out the target, intent only on draining all of the blood from their victim.

Places

Kodan decimated great swarths of the forest closest to Ebb's home by pushing Plasma into the roots of the trees. *While I managed to reverse the worst of the damage, it may be worth returning to check how they are faring.*

Iabovar

A Grey Realm of the second band, home to the stunning Niverwell Ranges.

Places

Niverwell Ranges

A stunning mountain range on the Realm of Iabovar. The range has a myriad of tiny, naturally created holes going from one side of the range to the other. It allows for the static build-up of two Elements, creating a whistling noise. Local legends claim the noise is caused by the souls of the departed.

The **Chirea** used the Niverwell Ranges as their base camp whilst they attempted to attack Lissae. They were stopped by the thirteenth Altoriae.

Beings and Creatures

Dragons

Fiona has reported small dragons in the markets of the Niverwell Ranges. No larger than the palm of her hand, it kept hold of a golden coin. It was able to breathe fire, and presumably had some sort of rudimentary brain, as it could understand her. Although she only saw the one, there may be more. Keep an eye out next time a patrol goes through.

Harvvens

A race inhabiting the Niverwell Ranges, on the Realm of Iabovar.

Ruzayra

A large, flightless bird with cloven feet. Able to walk great distances over mountainous terrain, the ruzayra are highly prized for its meat and feathers.

Karara

A Grey Realm of the second band that contains a xarit that leads to Xaviour.

Kilgaroth

A Grey Realm of the third band.

Lamink

A Grey Realm of the second band.

Libertatia

A Grey Realm of the second band. Home to pirates from across the Realms, Libertatia is regularly patrolled, although its gateway is rarely opened.

Luerix

A Grey Realm of the third band with monolithic standing stones ring the gateway.

Beings and Creatures

Sky Mother
A gigantic whale who rides currents of Plasma through the sky.

Maru

A Grey Realm of the third band. Currently has a bug problem. The sun struggles to make it through the perpetually foggy sky. The air is damp, which can cause breathing difficulties for those not used to it.

There were three basic types of Innarn available to the beings of Maru—Life, Fire, and Death Innarn, which they call Beyond.

Beings and Creatures

Beyonder

An Innarnian who leads the dead beings of Maru to their final resting place.

Maruians

Bipedal beings native to Maru. Typically, there are two distinct genders, with females wearing long skirts, and men in pants. Both wore long sleeves and high necks, although the clothing offered little in protection of anything bar the elements.

Geo

Innkeeper on Maru.

Glacia

Old woman who stayed at the Inn.

Souls

The souls of the departed travel with the pull of the moons and the sea, and eventually, they sink to the bottom of the ocean seeking peace until they are released to their final resting place by a **Beyonder**.

Food and Drink

Wheat-slab
Slice of bread.

Items

Focus stones
Stones imbued with Life, Fire, or Death Innarn. Each stone helps to focus a particular type of Innarn. Death stones will grow cold and glow when used. Life stones will grow lighter and pulse with a gentle light. Fire stones will dull and heat, feeling like warm coal.

Places

Grayvale
A town in Maru.

Shrine
Kept by a crone who could give Oalark a run for her years.

Words

Three-Stoner
Refers to a being who can use all three focus stones. Considered a very rare ability.

Mid Canak

A Grey Realm of the second band, which is one sub-level lower than Lissae. Mid Canak is organised by townships. A ridge of mountains runs around the entrance gateway. The beings here are segregated to their towns, typically the one they grew up in. Few choose to travel, as they do not have beasts of burden, or the tenacity to walk the distance required. The towns are walled and guarded by men... not all of whom are terribly competent.

Their advertising is often garish and wrong. The beings on this Realm are fierce defenders.

Places

Azmine's Ridge

A place on Mid Canak which is close to the entry to Lissae.

Bargavudh

A city eight days of trekking away from the Gateway. Surrounded by massive stone walls. Two guards are deployed at the city gates, dressed in plate armour, with a red and white tunic bearing a stylised beast on their chests.

Jorise's Inn

Found in Bargavudh. A copper plaque on the low fence bears the name "Jorise's Inn." The Inn has many rooms for guests to stay in, including the Garden Room, Music room, and Twilight room.

Beings and Creatures

Nacans

Tripedal beings who call Mid Canak home. Stout bodies, thick limbs and fingers, Nacans range from 4'5" to 7' tall. They are strict vegans.

Jorise

Potions master, host and owner of Jorise's Inn in Bargavudh. Brother of Gilsman.

Gilsman

Ruler of Bargavudh. Brother of Jorise.

Philna

Gilsman's wife. Beloved of Jorise.

Rapshider

Guard of Bargavudh's gates.

Rujin

Guard of Bargavudh's gates.

Wall Jumpers

Beings who cross the borders of Bargavudh without the appropriate paperwork.

Items

Cyfacide

A deadly potion. Taking approximately a week for a skilled potions' master to make, the black liquid will smoke and curdle, looking like overheated sludge when prepared correctly.

Flora

Rosin bloom

A plant growing in the jungle surrounding Bargavudh's walls. Favoured by the ruler of Bargavudh.

Nanka

A Grey Realm of the second band. Home to billions of beings, this futuristic Realm has buildings that brush the sky and glowing neon lights on their walls.

Neharn

A Grey desert Realm of the second band with two suns.

Beings and Creatures

Sinfrons

Creatures who can use Fire Innarn. The travel in packs and are able to catch up with even the fastest flying Ilturi. To avoid being roasted, it is suggested that beings who visit Neharn only walk instead of fly.

Nittany

A Grey Realm of the third band with a forest around its gateway.

Piltarn

A Grey Realm of the second band.

Beings and Creatures

Dragons

The sentient creatures with four limbs and wings, Dragons rule Piltarn with an iron claw and will fiercely defend their realm from infiltrators.

This particular race is thought to be the basis for all the dragon–like creatures on the Light and Grey Realms, including those who breathe fire, acid, and a host of other unpleasant breath–weapons.

Notes

Patrol at your own risk — they will breathe fire first and ask questions later

Permian

A Grey Realm of the third band.

Pet'hur

A Grey Realm of the second band, laid to waste by Altantian machines.

Ponton

A Grey Realm of the second band, two sub-levels higher than Lissae.

Beings and Creatures

Bone warriors
see **Chirea**.

Chirea
Originally from Ponton, the Chirea are a non-Innarnian race who strip the bones of their fallen enemies to make their armour, weapons, and occasionally structures for the never ending war they are fighting.

The Chirea show status and power through the amount of bone armour they have collected. They use golden arrows soaked in a special mixture created by the Q'Aralide to steal Innarn.

They are also known for poisons and soaking their weapons in potions that make healing by Innarn impossible. The Chirea made their base camp at Iabovar, near the Niverwell Ranges until they were defeated by the thirteenth Altoriae and Banished to Zokleran.

Luttrell

Of the Chirea. Former leader. Defeated by Amara of Lissae, *then by Nerina of the Usda. Take that, you big bonehead. Maybe if you respected females a bit more, they'd stop killing you. Oh, wait...*

Rilite

A Grey Realm of the third band.

Beings and Creatures

Strilite

A race from the Grey Realm of **Rilite**.

Riomache

A Grey Realm of the third band. A level below Lissae, their gateway opens out onto a desert city square.

Rumi

A Grey Realm of the first band.

Beings and Creatures

Assassin

An unnamed Rumi assassin tries to kill Shari Dawn in the Spring on 4059.

Shunar

A Grey Realm of the third band, home to blue-skinned cyclopes.

Beings and Creatures

Buthari

Blue-skinned cyclopes who guard Shunar. They bleed purple.

Oriaelle

Leader of the Buthari. Favoured a sword. Deceased at the claws of Oalark.

Suttporia

A Grey Realm of the first band. The gateway opens into perfect fields of blue grass.

Sentinel

Ellora
Of the Ducibus. Friend of Mitchel.

Tuklopia

A Grey Realm of the third band, where Guardian Jonathan Buan was ambushed in an attack that many thought took his sight.

Upper Bantaris

A Grey Realm of the first band.

Vinneča

A Grey Realm of the third band.

Places

Beings and Creatures

Falkirut
of Vinneča. Short, squat, slimy grey beings.

Vladine
Refugees from the Grey Realm of **Vinneča**, now living on Lissae.

Vutolea

A Grey Realm of the third band. Home of the Joratre.

Beings and Creatures

Cherill

Tall, furry primates with big brown eyes, long limbs and very long claws. These violent primates took over the forests near the gateway. One slash from their claws can lead to a nasty infection.

Joratre

A race native to Vutolea. Of Amazonian build, the Joratre have jet-black skin and live in polyamorous relationships.

Anthea

The Joratre giant has midnight-dark skin and a blinding white smile. An ally of the thirteenth Altoriae. Anthea has a harem of wives, and will regularly try to convince me to join them. When visiting with the Guild, she almost added Amara to her spouses.

Nalparak

Massive, antlered beasts native to Vutolea. The Joratre use them as both mounts and meat, depending on the sub-breed. Riding the Nalparak into battle is a sight to behold, and you'd want to be on the back of one, rather than in the army facing them down. They will not hesitate if urged by their rider, and have trampled more than one invading force.

Xaviour

A neutral Grey Realm of the second band where the preferred type of warning system is insects.

Beings and Creatures

Uallmi

An insect whose noise can burst humanoid eardrums. They spit acid if anything other than their own kind gets too close to them. They live in a cave on **Xaviour**. One of the ways to tell if the uallmi are close is yellow slime. The best way to get past the uallmi is to cover yourself in their slime and move the same way they do.

Xteria

A Grey Realm of the second band.

Notes

Asterion found a diary mentioning the realm — something about it growing and the dead coming back to life?

Zokleran

The Grey Realm of the first band where the Chirea were banished.

Dark Realms

Altum

A Dark Realm of the third band. Home to the Q'Aralide. They hosted the last Dark Conclave before a catastrophic event caused the collapse of Altum, leaving banished Q'Aralide scattered throughout the Realms with no hope of returning home.

Now destroyed

Beings and Creatures

Datzal

A Grey shapeshifting race conquered by the Q'Aralide and used as spies by the queen. Can move in the shadows and transform into anything they see. Natural form appears as a malnourished bipedal being. Rumoured to be from the Ninth Realm of Hell.

Fleqityls

Bugs that can get under the scales of a Q'Aralide. The only cure is an acid bath.

Q'Aralide

(said Que-*ral*-die) – A vicious Dark race who wield Spirit, Earth, Plasma, and Air Innarn. Approximately 30 feet tall, their social status depends more on their colour and abilities than anything else. They have black blood and forked tongues, and their saliva is acidic. Apart from their Innarn, their breath is something to watch out for, as it can strip the flesh and the life from someone in just one exhalation. Large, leathery wings allow for flight, and their third eye is said to be able to see things humanoids can't.

They are the Q'Aralide. They know no pain; they know no fear. Only hunger, anger, death, and the need to procreate. They are savage beings, as deadly as they are beautiful. Perhaps that makes their actions worse. They are ruthless. They will kill without thought for food, consequence, or soul, whether it be their victim's or their own.

The colours of the Q'Aralide scales indicate certain things. Generally, the lighter the scales, the older the creature. Red and its like are for warriors. Purple and metals_that is, gold, silver, bronze and the like_are for mages. Green and its like are for hunters. But be warned, any mixture may occur.

There are only ever sixty Q'Aralide at any time, and only ever one of each colour. It is believed they have between two and three times the maximum population waiting on their hatching grounds, which are found on their home Realm of Altum. They are master wielders of Spirit, Earth, Plasma, and Air Innarn.

"Never trust one, never love one, and never let one live."
-Fiona MacAde

Oalark

~~Queen~~ of the Q'Aralide. *Never did a being deserve a spear through the chest more than this one! Not my queen. Could she not have mentioned her life force was tied with Altum? A little warning would have been nice. Still not sad she's gone. May she turn in her grave, knowing I am in charge of the future of the Q'Aralide race.*

War'Jan

White male elder. Former leader of the Q'Aralide. Now deceased. *May he rot in the bowels of the Altum beast for all eternity*

Anjeler

Sapphire-coloured female. Priest. *Deceased*

Augur

Chestnut-coloured female. Field Commander. *Deceased*

Belos

Turquoise-coloured female. Hunter. *Deceased*

Buakn

Jade-coloured female. Hunt Leader. *Deceased*

Cisrk

Indigo-coloured male. Hunter. Currently in hiding. Outcast.

Curtunkra

Ruby-coloured male. Apprentice Priest. *Deceased*

Cuan

Violet-coloured male. Warrior. *Deceased*

Diren

Russet-coloured male. Warrior. Whereabouts unknown.

Divikin

Cobalt-coloured male. Warrior, Second in Command. *Deceased*

Drubaic
Navy-coloured male. Warrior. *Deceased*

Enark
Black-coloured male. Warrior Leader. *Deceased*

Faprak
Sandy-coloured female. Warrior. *Deceased*

Farnder
Cream-coloured female. Leader of the Hunters. *Deceased*

Gaster
Scarlet-coloured female. Warrior. *Deceased*

Gazn
Crimson-coloured female. Warrior. Deceased Q'Aralide. *I deeply regret your passing, my friend*

Helk
Vermilion-coloured male. Master Warrior. *Deceased*

Heseth
Silver-coloured Q'Aralide who became Head Priest after Sanithane left. *Deceased*

Honvic
Jet-black-coloured female. Q'Aralide hatchling. *Deceased*

Hurm
Dun-coloured female. Warrior. *Deceased*

Izarrk
Buff-coloured female. Leader of the Q'Aralide Priests. Sanithane's mentor. *Deceased*

Istaniern
Pearl-coloured female. Heseth's replacement as Head Priest. *Deceased*

Jaileth

Bronze-coloured female. Priest. Sanithane's mate. *Deceased*

Jaridran

Coral red-coloured female. Warrior. *Deceased*

Jayarn

Jet-coloured female. Warrior Leader. *Deceased*

Kirn

Rosy-coloured warrior. Killed by Cuan.

Knura

Navy Blue. Warrior. Whereabouts unknown. Kin to Samuel. *Saying 'whereabouts unknown' is kinder than 'could be lying dead somewhere' don't you think?*

Kowler

Amber-coloured male. Priest. *Deceased*

Kirjs

Light grey-coloured female. Hunter. *Deceased*

Likern

Fawn-coloured male. Warrior. *Deceased*

Ludok

Tan-coloured male. Warrior. *Deceased*

Matus

Khaki-coloured male. Hunt Leader. *Deceased*

Moxor

Coral pink-coloured female. Warrior. *Deceased*

Nasindr

Off-white-coloured male. Hunter. *Deceased*

Norle
Charcoal-coloured female. Warrior, Second in Command. *Deceased*

Nozro
Red-coloured male. Warrior. *Deceased*

Nukra
Tannin-coloured male. Hunter. *Deceased*

Orean
Carroty-coloured female. Warrior. *Deceased*

Pler
Cherry-coloured male. Warrior. *Deceased*

Punta
Purple-coloured female. Priest. *Deceased*

Qaster
Lavender-coloured male. Priest. *Deceased*

Qudrak
Mauve-coloured female. Warrior. *Deceased*

Raluva
Q'Aralide hatchling. Died by the claws and jaws of War'Jan.

Rataeo
Formerly of Altum. Izarrk's fated partner. Golden Priest before Sanithane. Created a Realm. See **Rataeo**.

Rikarn
Azure-coloured male. Leader of the Warriors. *Deceased*

Ruker
Navy blue-coloured male. Warrior. *I deeply regret your passing, my friend*

Sargorl
Puce-coloured female. Warrior. *Deceased*

Trugan

Ochre-coloured male. Warrior. *Deceased*

Tufa

Q'Aralide hatchling. Died by the claws and jaws of Oalark.

Tufar

Blue-coloured female. Head Priest. Disfavoured by Oalark. *Deceased*

Tunur

Pink-coloured male. Warrior. *Deceased*

Ularh

Orange-coloured female. Warrior. *Deceased*

Vaklar

Yellow-coloured female. Warrior. *Deceased*

Velkn

Ivory-coloured male. Leader of the Hunters. *Deceased*

Vice

Crimson-coloured female. Warrior. Deceased Q'Aralide.

Wolkrn

Maroon-coloured female. Warrior. *Deceased*

Xolket

Grey-coloured male. Warrior Trainer. *Deceased*

Yakel

Emerald-coloured male warrior. *Deceased*

Yassr

Olive-coloured female. Hunter. *Deceased*

Zedith

Green-coloured female. Hunter. Currently in hiding. Outcast.

Zeefron

Tawny-coloured female. Warrior. *Deceased*

Food and Drink

Dudrodie eggs

If these eggs have been incubated within the Q'Aralide Queen, they can cure **Grytycide** poisoning.

Grytycide

A deadly poison with only two cures—removing it from the victim's system or ingesting Dudrodie eggs.

Shemmegote Stinger

A smoking, green alcohol that Sanithane is partial to.

Items

Soul-seeker arrow

Once upon a time, there was a Dark Priest who created the perfect weapon to destroy Innarn on the bequest of his elder. He created a mixture that when an arrow of iron was doused with it, it would turn golden, and be able to transfer the Innarn from one to another. The elder insisted that the soul-seeker arrow be tested and used it to steal the Innarn from the Dark Priest's mate, attempting to take it for himself. The Innarn of another turned the elder mad, and the Dark Priest fled before the elder could take his Innarn as well.

Religion

Cylanthar

The Q'Aralide deity of destiny. She makes her presence known by the ringing of bells when events which have the potential to change her disciples' lives occur.

Cylanthar's Bells

The ringing of Cylanthar's Bells happens when events which have the potential to change her disciples' lives occur. See **Cylanthar**.

Ritual of the Third Moon, The

Occurs every thousand years, when a third moon graces Altum's skies. On that night, the hatchlings shed their black hides to discover their destiny.

Places

Acid Falls

Stemming from the stomach of the great beast of Altum, it is traditional for hatchlings to cross the falls as a symbol of growth and the next stage of life. Not all survive the crossing.

Acid River

Flowing from the falls, the river cuts through Altum, separating the living quarters of the higher-ranked Q'Aralide from the others.

Great City

The final city on Altum which houses all the Q'Aralide.

Nest Room

Considered the safest place on Altum, the Nest Room is where the next generation of Q'Aralide lay in wait. The queen can lay clutches of two hundred eggs at a time, usually every hundred years or so. These eggs will remain dormant until they are needed.

The Wall

A black wall was erected to separate the living quarters of the lower-ranked Q'Aralide from where the Conclave would meet, or where prisoners would be kept in the years the Conclave would not run.

Map of Altum

Baenge

A Dark sentient Realm of the third band with a shell for a door. A giant turtle carries the Realm on its back.

Beings and Creatures

Sebbolen

A race of blue-skinned beings with pointed ears.

Coqi

A Dark Realm of the first band that makes your fears come true.

Beings and Creatures

Tuostinet

A creature as tall as three men with claws as long as a Lissaen adult's torso tipping each finger. Long, curved horns sit on either side of the cat-like head. Fur covers the four limbs and powerful body. Only the three toes at the end of each limb are hairless.

Cradamull

A Dark Realm of the second band. Oalark eats their elder during the Dark Conclave.

Beings and Creatures

Semaed

A dull, grey-skinned, quadrupedal creature who has the ability to pass through narrow spaces thanks to their thin frame.

Cuplith

A Dark Realm on the third band. *Don't drink the water. It will make even the strongest of beings violently ill.*

Beings and Creatures

Wastigg

A large beast with a body and head like a bull, and a scorpion's tail and claws. They stand on four feet, ten feet high at the wither/top of the shoulder.

Dakleozen

A Dark Realm of the third band.

Damiuth

A Dark Realm of the third band.

Beings and Creatures

Zanterians

A race from the Dark Realms.

Eazithan

A Dark Realm of the third band with a bristle hide-covered door with a bronze handle and hinges.

Beings and Creatures

Fulni

An animal similar to Earth's buffalo but carnivorous and with two heads. The last fulni herd went extinct over two hundred years ago. Their tails are attached to a major artery, and if the tail is removed, they will bleed out in seven seconds.

Anriluka ate the last herd, and they terrorised all who resided in her pocket Realm until her defeat.

Upon arrival at the new realm, the fulni were ushered into a pocket realm accessable only by rutenberry farmers.

Eofix

A Dark Realm of the second band home to huge beings.

Gihalan

A Dark Realm of the third band.

Beings and Creatures

Xanter

A humanoid race from the Dark Realms which uses Fire Innarn.

Hinioxar

A Dark Realm of the third band.

Beings and Creatures

Tu'zar

A cute, fluffy, bipedal species descended from apes, the Tu'zar generally inhabit the jungles of the Dark Realms. Their dark fur helps them to blend into the shadows. The most common marking is a 'mask' across their eyes.

Kintage

A Dark Realm of the third band.

Beings and Creatures

Belopod

Large quadrupedal beasts with huge shoulders and spines along their back. The spines excrete toxins into the air which poisons everything around them. They can be quite persistent when they want something and are happy protecting those who don't hurt or hunt them.

Perce

One of the Belopods from Anriluka's Pocket Realm. Named by Collis for his persistence.

Lefo

A Dark Realm of the first band that is said to have held the *Hekkor Mafae*.

Beings and Creatures

Korvie

A humanoid race from the Dark Realms who primarily uses Water Innarn.

Mishone

A Dark Realm of the second band which was burned down by the queen of the Q'Aralide when the previous chair of the Dark Conclave failed to report for his duties. The name has since been forgotten and the Realm erased from history

Morreth

A Dark Realm of the third band.

Beings and Creatures

Ne'fora

Generally considered amongst the most wise and venerable races of the Realms, the Ne'fora stick to telepathic communication as the instant they open their mouths unintelligible screaming comes out.

Nalbba

A Dark Realm of the third band.

Beings and Creatures

Retching hogs

Six-limbed creatures with short snouts which cover most of their faces. They are famous for the retching noise that consistently gives away their position to predators. Despite the sound, the meat is a sought-after delicacy.

Ninth Realm of Hell

A Dark Realm in the third band.

Obirim

A Dark Realm of the third band with a door of deep black wood that seems to glow.

Beings and Creatures

Camor

A large, quadrupedal species with a hump on its back and short, thick legs. Camor flesh is prized in the Dark Realms and is considered a delicacy in some of the Grey Realms. Thick skin protects its sides and back. Although it is said to make one of the saddest calls in all the Realms when dying, only certain races can hear the noise due to the pitch.

Otike

A Dark Realm of the third band.

Beings and Creatures

Gourhog

Large, horned, pig-like creatures with spines running along their backs. Typically, the extra-strong backbone and ribcage are enlarged on gourhogs and lay just underneath the skin. Difficult to kill without getting ripped apart.

Otike

Green-skinned giants with prominent under-tusks, clawed fingers, and knuckles from the Dark Realm sharing the same name.

Zirgha

Ambassador of **Otike**.

Panagar

A Dark Realm of the third band with a metal door.

Beings and Creatures

Yrusri

A race from the Dark Realms.

Pezium

A Dark Realm of the second band.

Beings and Creatures

Denfur
A race of gelatinous beings.

Items

Hydrusfel
Toxic substance from the upper Grey Realms that can be used to poison those from the Dark Realms.

Ralera

A Dark Realm of the first band.

Beings and Creatures

Hanotqe
A short, squat being whose large skull holds a significant amount of fat and very little brain.

Jalbobvesi
Tiny, squirming, flesh-eating insects. Shari received a thigh wound from these bugs.

Food and Drink

Pulmattan
A sweet fruit. A favourite of Temira's.

Rataeo

A Dark ice Realm of the second band, virtually uninhabited, on which the time speed is double Lissae's. He is home to the U'tan. Most of the animals are relatively harmless, except for the metsari.

Places

Planomest

A sacred area on Rataeo that is used for rites and rituals. It has a labyrinth of tunnels and caves and is home to a large group of metsari.

Beings and Creatures

Metsari

A small, reptilian animal from Rataeo that spits poison to protect their territory. They also have a very eerie call, which sounds like a cross between a high-pitched whistle and a wolf howling. They usually live in packs of ten or more. There is a sacred area on Rataeo where the largest grouping of metsari lives, called Planomest. The only way to avoid the metsari is to not touch the ground. When they feel vibrations through their bodies, they spit poison. The only cure for their poison is to lick it off.

Pteradiles

Reptilian birds with poisonous claws. A favourite snack of the **U'tan**.

Sedolic

Green, scaly, dog-like animals with two large pincers at their front. They are a favoured food of the **U'tan**.

U'tan

The U'tan are famous for planning every attack out in minute detail, with contingency plans for everything they could think of. Of course, this often means that the creature they plan to attack has died of old age before they get to it, but the U'tan would consider that a victory as well.

Composed mostly of tentacles and menace, this is not a race to mess with. Sporting beak-like mouths and hooks on their tentacles, U'tan's are quite adept at rending the flesh from their intended victims. They bleed purple.

Tentacle closeup

Note the barbed hooks

Beak-like mouth

Anriluka

This U'tan is older than Lissae's calendar. She almost devoured Ronah's entire population before Muran Curtis' Guardian banished her back to her home Realm. Anriluka was finally defeated by Shari Dawn, the thirteenth Altoriae, in the spring of 4059.

Glad she's gone. Ugh.

Note the swelling behind her head—current theory: U'tans with a pocket Realm will have the same sort of swelling.

Raval

A Dark Realm of the second band reduced to cinders at the hands of the largest Dark Army ever seen.

Beings and Creatures

Fempar

A creature the size of a medium dog, it had six legs, antennas, and it was the only thing on the Realms that could pierce a Q'Aralide hide. Now extinct.

Roefill

A Dark Realm of the third band.

Beings and Creatures

Ashbek

Elder of Roefill.

Saundun

A Dark Realm of the third band. Home to the famous crystal forest.

Items

Isoiglabrane

A powerful aphrodisiac made from the crushed leaves of the crystal forest.

Places

Crystal Forest

Made entirely of growing crystal, the forest is home to many trees, each of which produces a different use.

Strozna

A Dark Realm of the third band.

Teroupi

A Dark Realm of the first band.

Beings and Creatures

Kedjum

Native to Teroupi, the kedjum is a wild, tangled, and unpredictable ball of fluff and teeth. Don't be fooled by the sweet, innocent appearance. The average kedjum will spend its life in the trees, waiting for unsuspecting creatures to walk past. That's when they'll strike, opening the sweet smile to reveal rows of razor-sharp teeth while vine-like limbs wrap around you to prevent escape.

Don't pet it!

Tiaclorune

A Dark Realm of the third band.

Beings and Creatures

Feseor

Often used as a curse word and refers to ravenous creatures that live in scum-filled ponds.

Ulnan

Places
Noxeomyth

A type of sauna on Ulnan that uses acidic fumes instead of steam.

Beings and Creatures
Ucoid

A small, annoying, blood-sucking insect native to Ulnan.

Ulanians

Tall, blue-skinned beings exceptionally talented at Blood, Crystal, and Techno Innarn.

Temira

Sole survivor. Now of Talhan. See **Temira** (under Beings of Lissae).

Vitaemancers

A type of Innarnian found on Ulnan who can control the blood inside another being or creature, dictating their every move. Vitaemancers can also cure diseases and successfully treat blood conditions.

Rituals

The Ulanians eat the bodies of their dead in order to honour the cycle of life. While off-putting for other beings, to be eaten is considered the highest honour a Ulanian can be bestowed.

Vastilda

A Dark Realm of the third band with an ice door. Its inhospitable cold weather made it the perfect place to hide the *Hekkor Mafae*.

Beings and Creatures

Iomnuroz

A creature with razor-sharp claws.

Vastildian cyclops

A variant of cyclops who have four arms, the Vastildian's seemed to have preferred limbs to brains.

Vennph

A particularly Dark Realm of the third band home to the Wikkur and formerly to the Eni.

Beings and Creatures

Eni

Malicious shapeshifters, able to permanently assume the form of influential figures to summon others of their kind to possess the subjects they have gained. Seriously Dark beings, the Eni are not often seen out of the Dark Realms. The Eni mentally 'piggyback' their prey before assuming their form. They were wiped out by the thirteenth Altoriae during an unsuccessful attempt to take over Lissae.

Wikkur

A savage, brutal race. They can claim amongst their numbers some of the best warriors and leaders in the Realms.

Usually standing at 6 feet tall, the Wikkur have three legs, a stout body, two arms and one head. The only other physically unusual feature about this race is their extra set of eyes, which are located slightly behind their small ears. These eyes remain closed most of the time, and the Wikkur have to make a conscious choice to view the world through them. They bleed clear plasma, rather than red blood.

The Wikkur exist on many Dark and Middle Realms, with their home Realm being that of Vennph, located in the Dark Realms.

The Wikkur are able to use basic Innarn but seem uninterested as a race in furthering their skills.

Gulan

A Wikkur. One of the Returned who was shifted off Lissae as soon as he arrived.

Vi

A Wikkur of ill intent.

Vikthasi

A Dark Realm of the third band.

Beings and Creatures

Grui

A female who failed to seduce a Q'Aralide.

Viorath

A Dark Realm of the first band.

Beings and Creatures

Knarec

Acclaimed archers with arrows strong enough to hurt a Q'Aralide.

Yettara

A Dark Realm of the third band that resides in perpetual darkness and is one of the few Realms that have a black sky. Its time speed is five times slower than Lissae's. It is sentient and feeds off any creature from the Light or Grey Realms who come to visit. Only the strongest creatures from the Lighter Realms can survive there. Any magic from a creature of the Light or Grey Realms that is performed there will be unlikely to succeed in doing anything but draining the being further. The prolonged stay of creatures from the Light or Grey Realms on Yettara is guaranteed to end in death.

Beings and Creatures

Ullfin

Herd creatures. Large rhinoceros-like beasts with scaly hides and long, drooping ears. Jali Thorne, the tenth Altoriae, was killed by a trampling herd of the creatures when trying to save her family.

Zoiban

A Dark Realm of the second band home to mammoth sea creatures.

Places

Bolka Volcano

An active volcano. Home to the teifnols.

Beings and Creatures

Nossan

Mammoth sea creatures.

Teifnols

Beings who roam the side of the Bolka Volcano. Their hides are so thick that they allow the outer layer to become charred in order to protect the inner hide.

Zooghe

A Dark Realm of the third band.

Beings and Creatures

Dofi

Native to the Dark Realms, the dofi are considered a delicacy. Small creatures with a grey, scaly body, long tentacles, and two enormous eyes, the dofi have limited intelligence. They are raised watching their parents get eaten and believe they will be reunited with their family in the stomachs of others.

WEAPONS

All these weapons and more are used throughout the Realms. This gives you a brief glimpse of what they may look like, and who has favoured them.

Axe

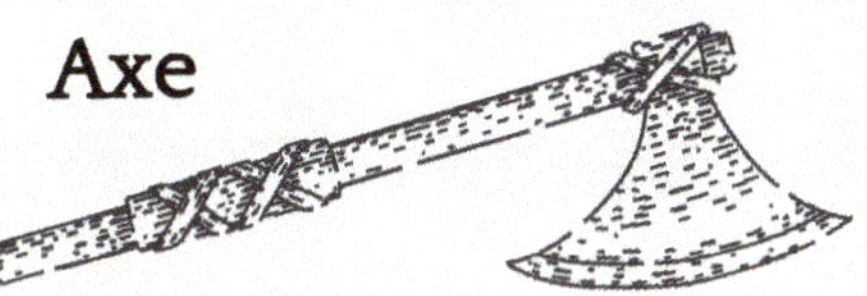

Battleaxe

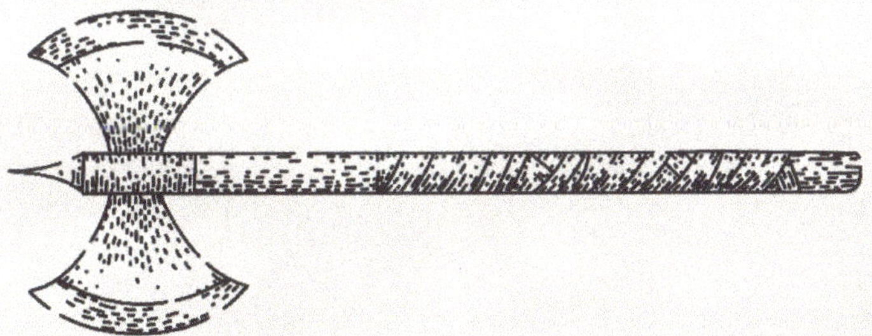

Great axe

Favoured by Amara of Lissae.

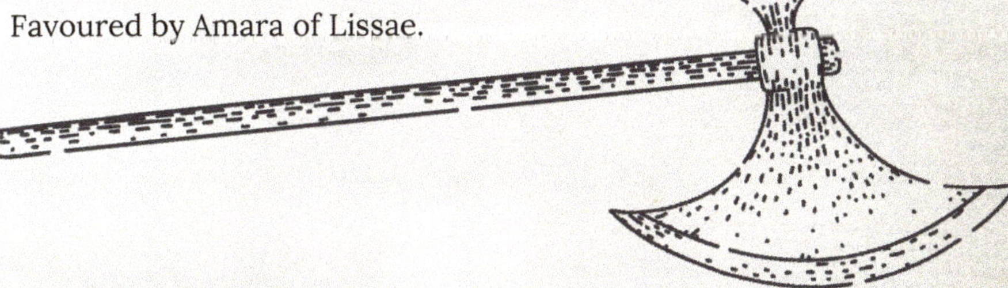

Throwing axe

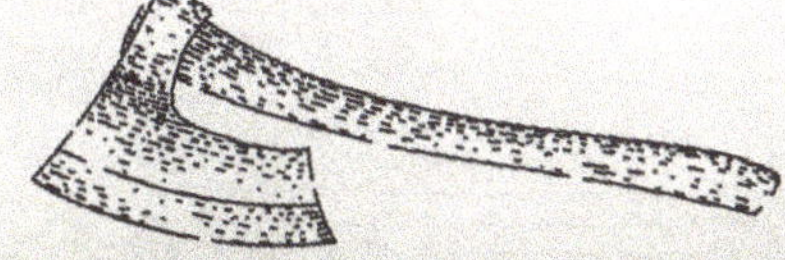

Chakram

A disk-like blade with a razor-sharp edge and a large hole in the centre. Only a few species use it as their preferred weapon. The Yoxant are one such species.

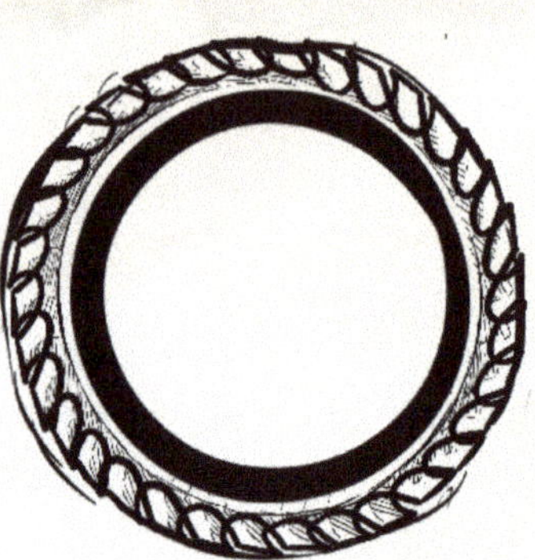

Bow

Favoured weapon of many, including Altoriae Kay'imi and candidate Esme.

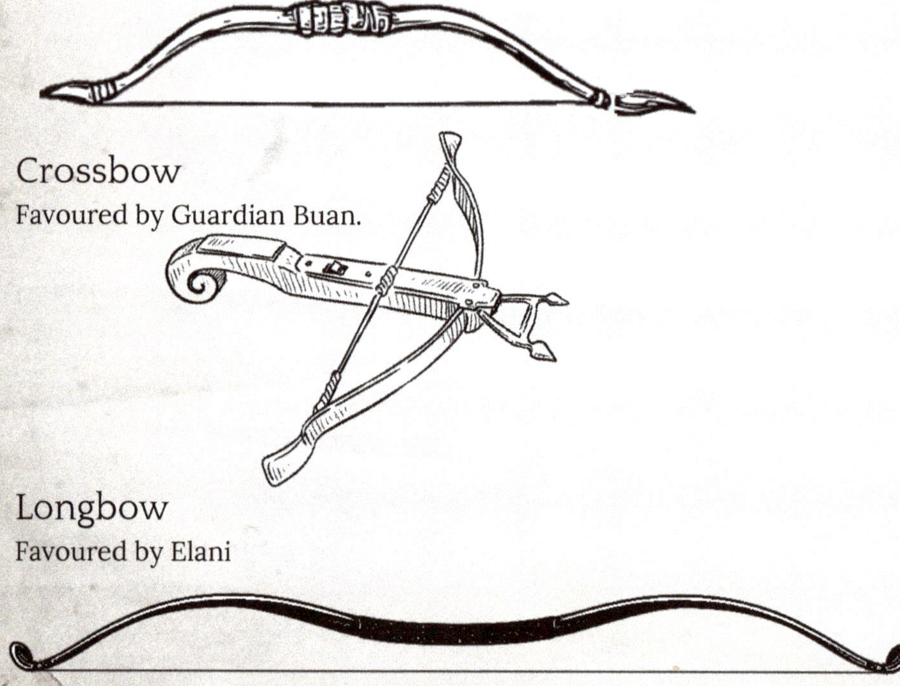

Crossbow

Favoured by Guardian Buan.

Longbow

Favoured by Elani

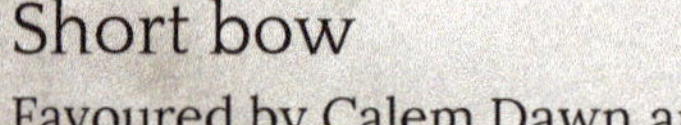

Short bow

Favoured by Calem Dawn and most Ilutri.

When Ilutri craft their arrows, they typically use feathers from their own wings.

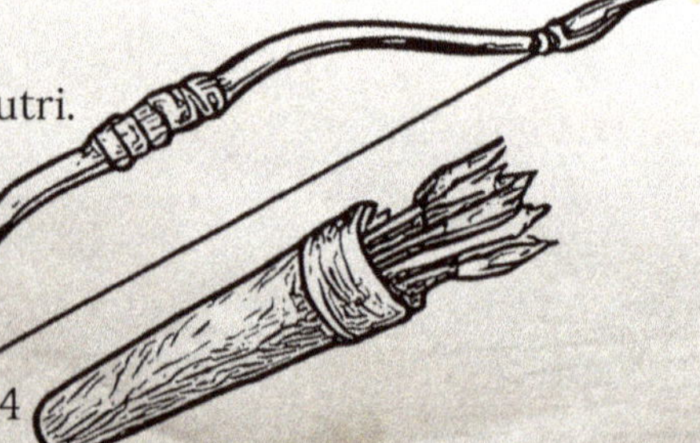

Club

Spiked cudgel

A spiked wooden club used by Ashlen of Ronah.

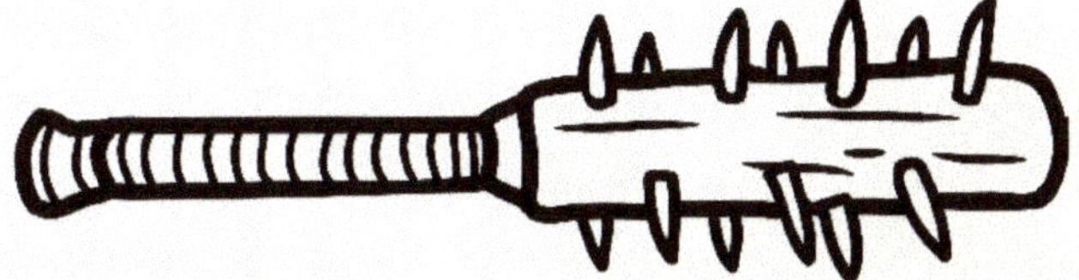

Dagger

Stiletto

Favoured weapon of Anika Thorne.

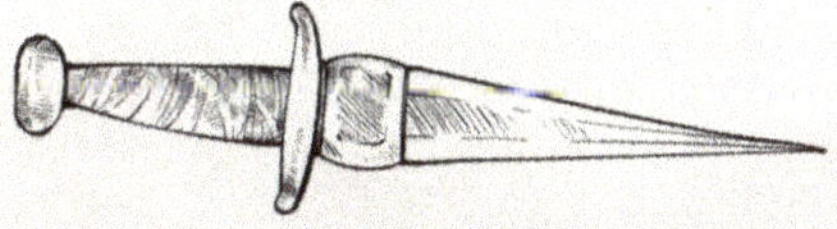

Throwing Knife

Favoured weapon of Guardian Neev

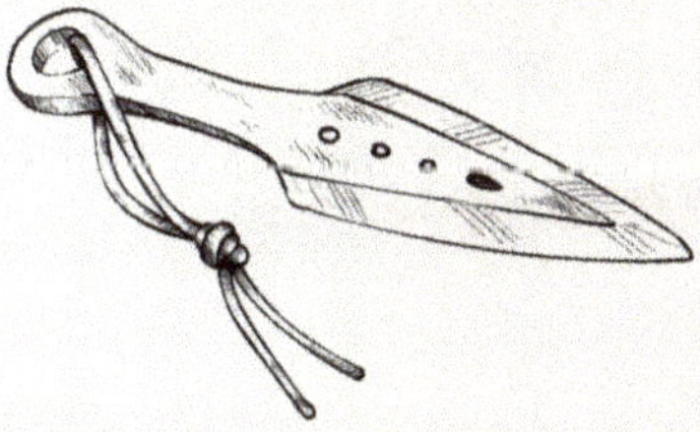

Glaive

Favoured weapon of Altoriae Crista.

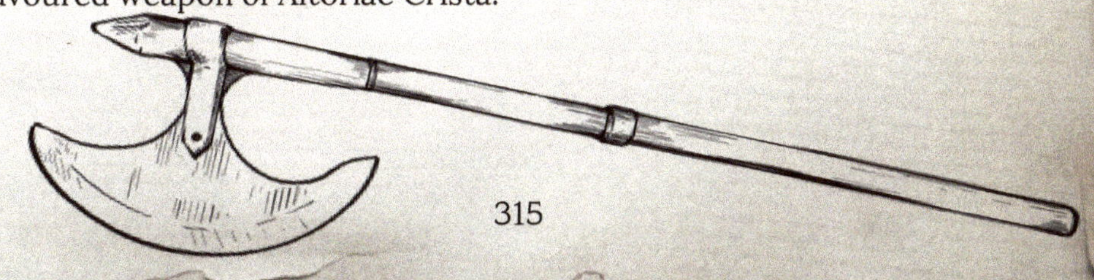

Halberd

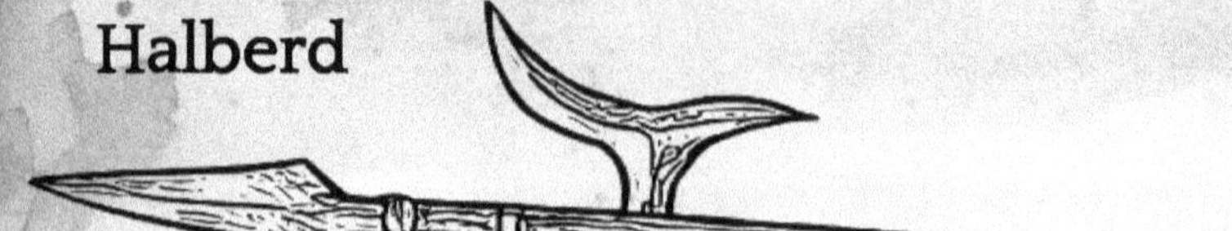

Mace

Flail

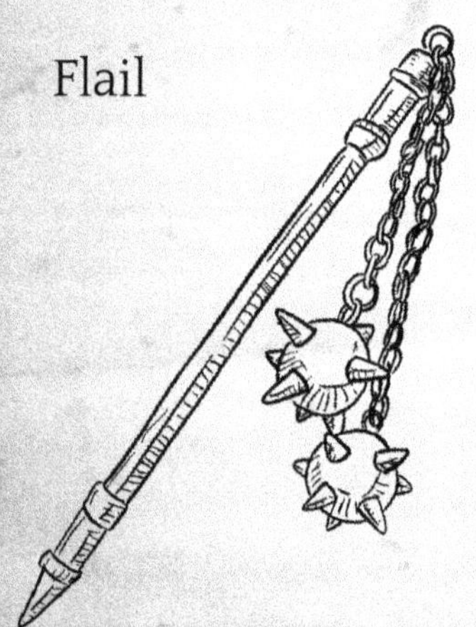

Poleaxe

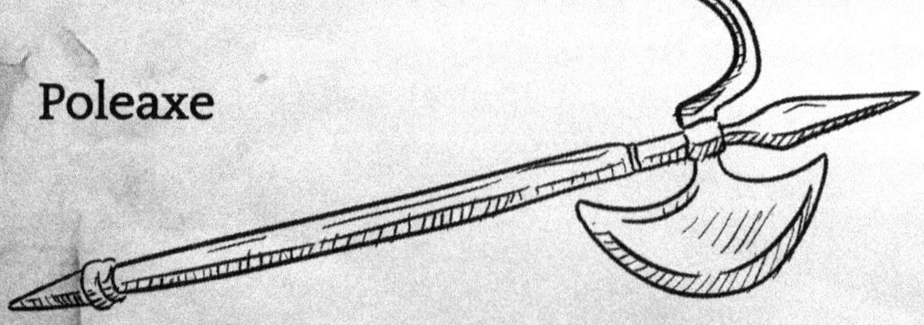

Quarterstaff

Favoured weapons of Altoriae Tanika and Guardian Joshua.

Rope

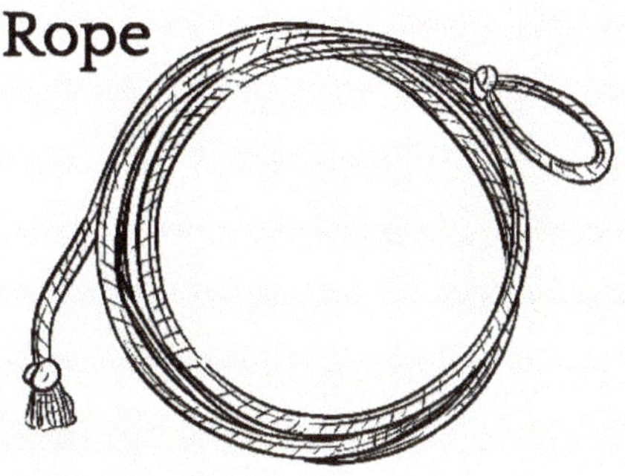

Scythe

The weapon that killed Altoriae Fiona MacAde.

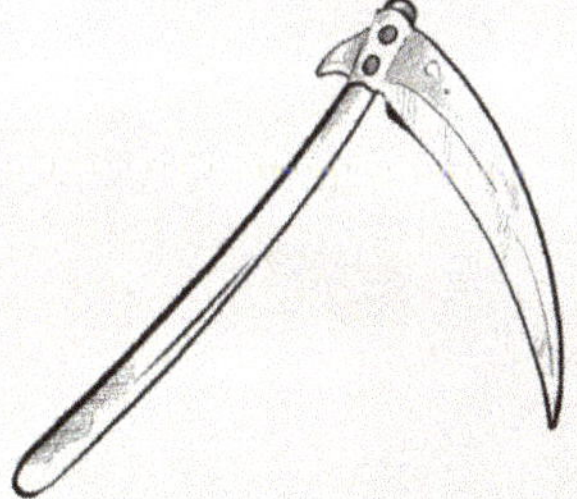

Shield

Not just used for defence, shields can also be used in bludgeoning attacks.

Sickle

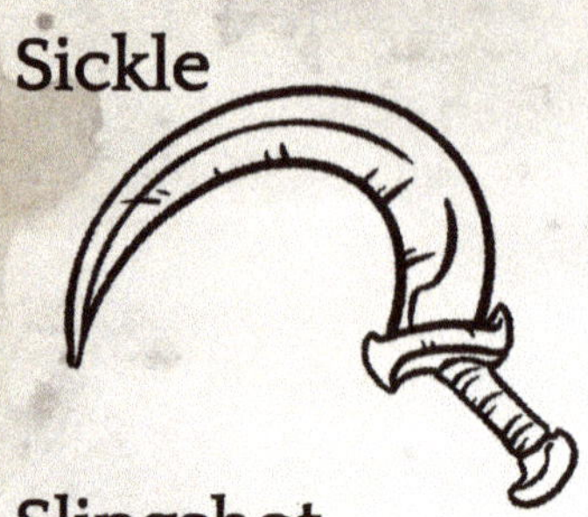

Slingshot

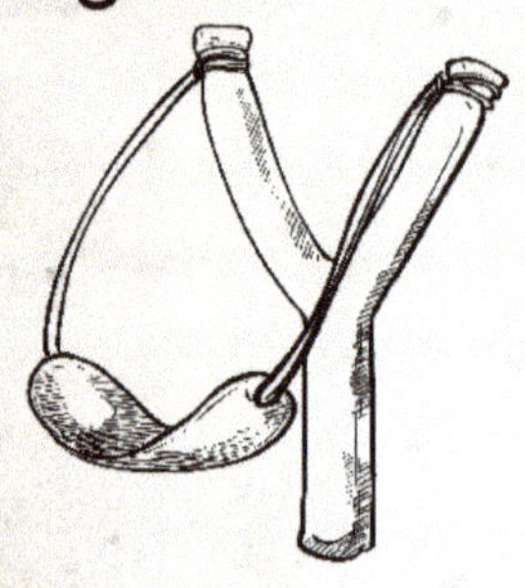

Spiked chain

Favoured weapon of Wubi of the U'sala.

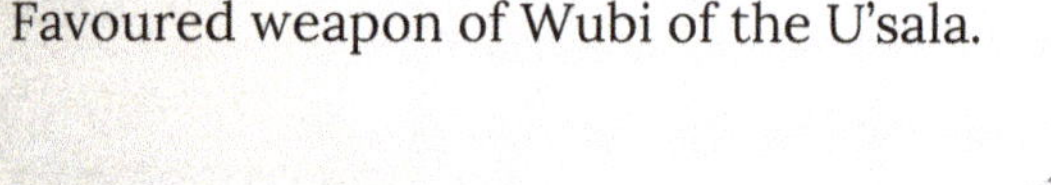

Sword

Favoured weapon of Arilla Dawn of Ronah.

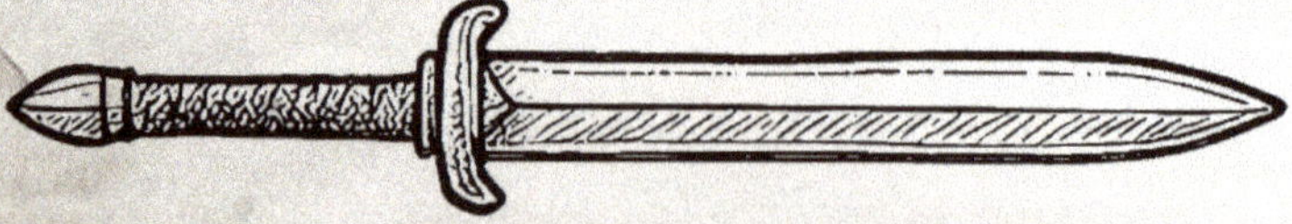

Longsword

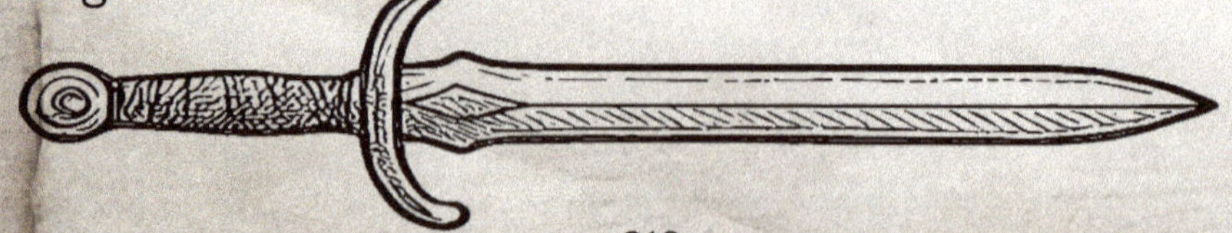

Shortsword

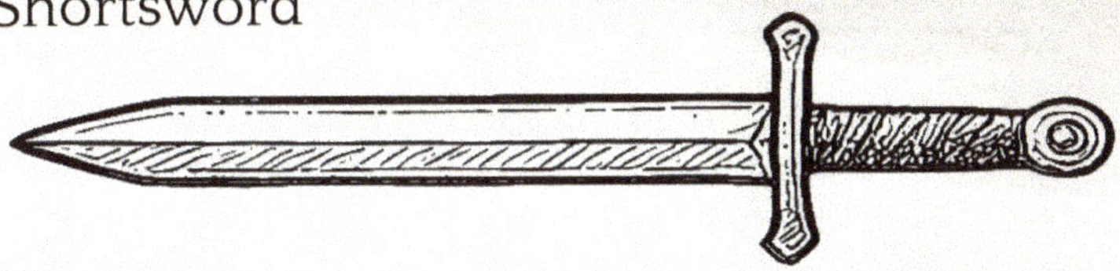

Saber

A short sword with a curved blade that broadens towards the point. Favoured weapon of Altoriae Shari.

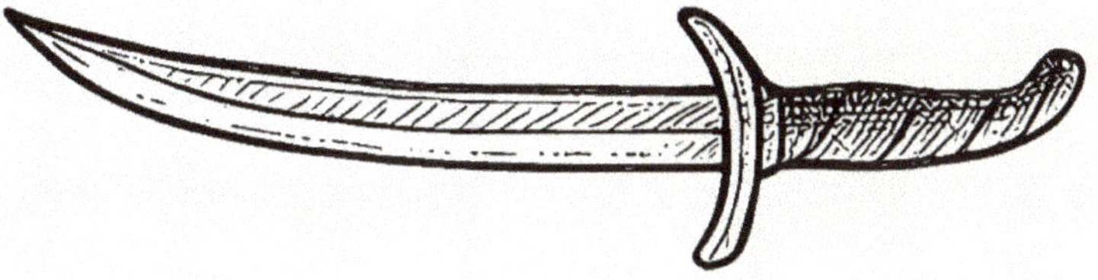

Trident

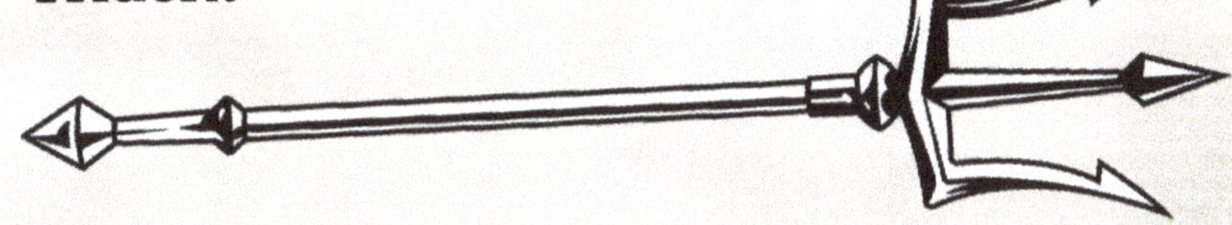

War Hammer

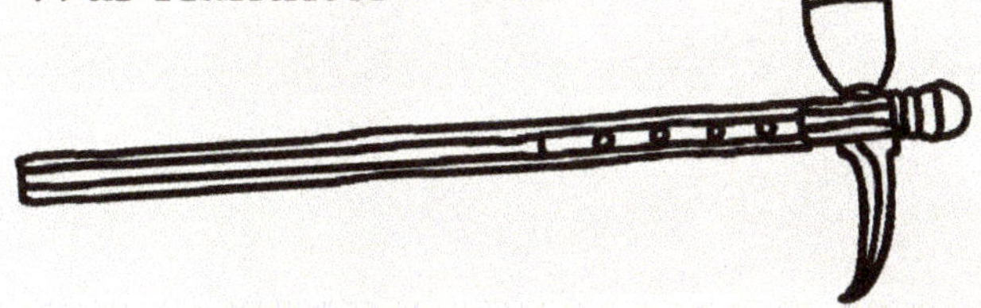

Double headed war hammer

Favoured weapon of Denesska of Ronah.

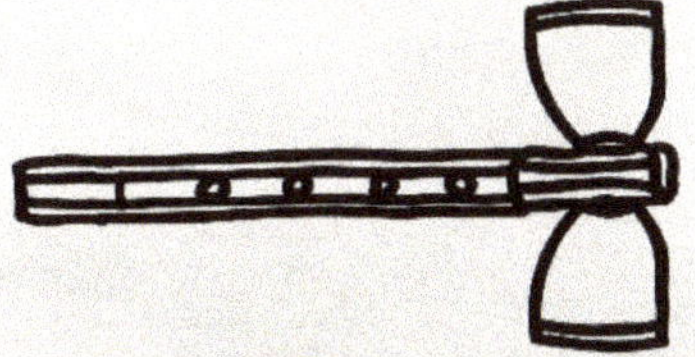

INDEX

This index is arranged alphabetically. Bold numbers indicate that is where the bulk of the information is. If you've come across something you are trying to look up, it should be listed alphabetically in the index.

Try as I might, I can not get the page numbers for the main Altoriae section to remain. Those, you'll have to read through yourself.

Best of luck, and may your journey through the realms be a safe one.

—Jonathan

A

B